Really well written. Zoë has a great sense for dialogue. For a first writing this is fantastic... truly. Kept me in suspense until the very end.

— TOM JACOBS

Zoë Pruden immerses the reader in the tender and anxious inner landscape of a young teen. Pruden skillfully builds suspense through fraught social interactions, her characters emerging through a mosaic of high school experiences. This is a writer to watch.

— HEATHER MCRAE-WOOLF

I look forward to her next work and imagining the writer she will become.

— RICHARD COX

The artists who impress me the most are those who have dedication to their craft through practice. Not only does Zoë have this in spades, she has a unique outlook and style that give her work a fresh perspective. It is so cool that she has written this book and I know her craft will continue to grow and shine.

— RICK MYERS

When I Left

WHEN I LEFT

A NOVELLA

ZOË PRUDEN

RP
FA
ross pruden
fine art

This is a work of fiction. Names, characters, places, and incidents either are the product of the author's imagination or are used fictitiously. Any resemblance to actual persons, living or dead, events, or locals is purely coincidental.

First edition: October 2022

Book design by Ross Pruden
Illustrations by Zoë Pruden

ISBN 978-1-956708-22-6 (hardback)
ISBN 978-1-956708-21-9 (paperback)
ISBN 978-1-956708-20-2 (eBook)

Published by Ross Pruden Fine Art
www.rosspruden.art
Sales inquires to ross@rosspruden.art

FOREWORD

When you first begin to write seriously, it's hard to know if what you've produced is any good. I know this from experience. At age eleven I was the only writer I knew personally, and that remained true until I took a creative writing course in college.

Even when you do know other authors, it can be scary to share your work. What if other people don't like it? How are you meant to improve?

In November 2020, when the COVID-19 virus was still unchecked by vaccines, I was introduced by Ross Pruden to his daughter, Zoë. Ross and I had been friends since Zoë was a tot. Now she was 13 years old and an aspiring author! She'd been writing for some time, in fact, and was about to embark on a new creative project for school. The goal was to produce a manuscript and a presentation about the process of writing. The project also called for a mentor, and Zoë wondered if I might be interested in that role.

Knowing how lonely and difficult the process can be, especially for a younger writer, I was excited to help. It was the kind of guidance I would have appreciated at a similar age. What I didn't know was Zoë's skill level or how she would respond to feedback about her work. After all, even adult authors can be sensitive to criticism... sometimes painfully so. And I also remembered my own writing skill at a similar age, which was modest by any measure.

But then Zoë sent me her first two chapters and I was blown away. I had imagined much of our time together would be to discuss grammar and syntax, but I soon realized her first draft was mature and polished in a way unusual for someone her age. Instead of writing basics, what Zoë was really looking for was guidance about more advanced concepts like plot structure and characterization. And of course the motivation to stay on schedule. My oldest daughter has herself just reached middle school, so I know how many distractions teenagers face in a culture dominated by social media and nonstop breaking news. Zoë and I spoke over FaceTime every two weeks. She was always open to suggestions and eager to implement them. Sometimes she sent me two or three chapters at a time. Sometimes only one. Sometimes she faced writer's block and other times her output was prodigious, but I was always impressed with her. In fact, the first bit of feedback I offered was this (yes, I used all caps): "YOU ARE AN AMAZING WRITER FOR YOUR AGE."

Over time we developed a rhythm to our conversations and my feedback for her. We structured the process similar to how an author might work with her editor. Some big changes in structure emerged from our conversations, and I encouraged her to pare her prose to the necessary elements. We discussed how certain characters behaved, what they knew and when they knew it, to ensure continuity and to ratchet up the suspense. Zoë even performed her own research about certain technological concepts. It was important that her work seem as believable as possible, which was impressive for a writer of her age. Everything about her was impressive.

As the project deadline loomed, as we worked through a second draft, Zoë grew more anxious, just like every author racing toward the end of her project. We started working line-by-line to fine-tune her style. We finished just before the deadline and both of us were thrilled with the final product. Her presentation—an 8th grade requirement along with the story itself—was a success as well. It was quite a ride!

Not every aspiring writer can be objective about her work. A lot of people with talent don't make it far because they're too precious with their ideas. Some don't see a difference between the best fiction and their own work. But those who learn to be objective, who are willing to hear criticism about their work, possess the potential to become successful authors themselves. And that's my opinion of Zoë Pruden. She has already produced work to be proud of, and no doubt she will continue to improve.

I enjoyed working with Zoë on *When I Left* and I think you will enjoy reading it, too. I look forward to her next work and imagining the writer she will become.

Good luck, Zoë, and thank you for being such a great writer and student.

Richard Cox
Tulsa, OK
December 15, 2021

Dedicated to the reader–

Because without you,
this wouldn't be possible.

Land without water... is still just land.
But water without land... is nothing at all.
—Unknown

PART 1

I

AFTER

And here I had let myself forget about Jonathan.

You know that feeling you get, when the world seems to flip upside down and you can't believe no one can hear your heartbeat? When you realize something's true, yet there's no way it can be? When it feels, *needs* to be a dream, but somehow... isn't?

That's how I felt when I saw Jonathan Sinclair.

I scanned the room for an exit, but the tables were filled with laughing students who would certainly notice the unfamiliar face standing in the middle of their cafeteria.

I felt eyes on me, the dark force in my gut tightening as my hands began to sweat. I stared at him, noticing the golden hair, thin frame, slight slouch of his back. It was all too familiar. He laughed, and then began to turn, kicking my heart into high gear as I snapped back to reality.

Move, I thought, stumbling forward mechanically. *Just keep your head down, don't look, find a—*

"Emily?"

I flinched, whipping around to see... a girl? She was pretty, blonde hair cascading over her shoulders, blue eyes looking up at me curiously.

"You're Emily, right?"

"Uh... yeah?"

"Okay, good!" she exclaimed. "Awkward situation avoided. I'm Clara."

"Why—uh... Hello?"

Clara laughed, walking over to an empty table and plopping into one of the seats. "Come on."

"Okay," I whispered, taking the seat next to her. I was grateful for the distraction, but confused nonetheless.

"Let's start over," Clara began, extending a hand. "Hi. I'm Clara Fallon, nice to meet you."

The way she spoke was captivating: quick, in control, and confident, clearly more comfortable in her skin than I'd ever be in mine. I shook hands with her briefly, hoping I'd stopped sweating. She didn't seem to notice.

"Hey. I'm Emily."

"Everyone already knows that," Clara said, taking a bite out of a large apple. "You're the new kid. Which is especially strange since you moved here in the *middle* of the year. What gives?"

I cringed inwardly—this was just getting better and better.

"No worries, though. In a week something even newer will come along. And anyways, I'm getting distracted," she laughed again. "Basically, what I'm trying to say is that I'm supposed to show you around, so any questions about anything," she paused to take another bite of the apple, "ask me."

"Thanks," I whispered, trying to focus, but Clara's words wouldn't stay in my head. Too much, too soon. My brain was already taxed enough. Considering what happened with Jonathan last year, considering what I'd done, the last thing I needed was more attention. Because the memories were always there, and always painful. Always a reminder.

"Oh, and sorry I couldn't find you before your first period, it is Monday after all, but I can help you find this one... Emily? Hello?"

What if it really is Jonathan? Could I be this unlucky? There were plenty of tall blonde boys in school, right?

"Emily? Hey, are you okay?"

"Huh?"

Jonathan this, Jonathan that.

Clara's brows knit together, her eyes darkening as she looked me up and down. "You don't look so good," she whispered, leaning closer. "Is everything okay?"

No.

"Yeah, I'm fine," I said, smiling faintly.

"Really?"

My heart began to speed up again, bringing back that hot fidgety feeling.

"No no no, everything's great."

Nobody could know. For everyone's sake, especially Mom's. She'd been through too much because of me. Calling it a traumatic experience would've been an understatement. I *couldn't* let that happen again.

What are you doing? I thought. *Stop. I need to stop.* I couldn't lose myself down that hole again.

"Actually," I said, "there *is* something."

"Yeah?"

"Well, I just got here, and we kinda moved to restart y'know? And I thought I saw this guy I knew, and everything came flooding back."

"Ex-boyfriend?" Clara asked.

"In a way. We didn't really end on good terms."

"I know exactly how you feel," Clara said, and I couldn't deny that I felt a little better than before. Yet, I was still lying to her.

"He was terrible and I guess I never really—y'know what? Let's not talk about this."

"Agreed."

We shared a smile, a real smile, the fidgety feeling disappearing if for only a moment.

"So," Clara said, "what's your next class again?"

"Science."

"Perfect, mine's French so we can just..." she paused, locking my gaze to hers. "Actually, there's some people I want you to meet —" She glanced behind me. "Mase! Nate! Come over here!"

I smiled, a warm feeling brushing through me as I twisted, but when I saw them, my heart kickstarted back to irregularity. Jonathan and his friend. Perfect. I'd have to act if I didn't want to get recognized. I'd always been a good *actor*.

Clara turned back to me with a grin on her face, like she expected me to thank her.

If only she knew.

Still I smiled, dragging my gaze to their faces. The dark-haired boy smiled back, before slipping into the seat next to mine.

"Mason Taylor," he said, extending a hand warmly. I glanced over at Clara, receiving an unhelpful grin, before turning back to Mason. His grip was firm and determined and when his hand left mine, it fell to his side. Mine stayed, feeling cold and empty.

"I'm... Emily," I squeaked, wincing at his soft laugh.

Clara smiled, yet it was short-lived as she turned to Jonathan, motioning with her eyes.

"Nate?"

"I'm Jonathan—Sinclair—but you can call me Nate," he said carefully, eyes narrowed ever so slightly. "Emily, right?"

2

AFTER

There it was. Jonathan Sinclair. The name I'd dreaded and tried my hardest to forget, to erase from all my memories, was now taunting me from less than a foot away.

"Yeah I—" I began, trying to look anywhere but Jonathan's calculating gaze. Luckily, I was saved by the ring of a bell. The sudden rush of students pierced into my head with a whine. *Ouch.*

"We should get to class," Clara said, popping to her feet. "See you guys in Bio?"

"Yeah, good luck!" Mason hollered as Clara reached the door, turning back to motion me over.

I practically ran to her, mumbling a goodbye to the boys, glad to be out of *that* situation.

"So... where's Science again?"

Clara laughed, grabbing me by the hand as she dove into the mess of students. With a sigh, and a look over my shoulder, I followed her.

By the number of twists and turns Clara took as we fought through the crowd, I knew I never would've found my way without her.

"Okay," Clara said, pausing in front of a classroom labeled *B305*. "I have to go, but good luck!"

Good luck? Again? What was this school...

I sighed, pushing open the door to reveal an ordinary classroom. Ordinary was something I really needed in this "new" life. Then again, I could never know if—

"Mr. Sinclair?" a voice said as the bell chimed. "You're late."

"Sorry," a familiar voice murmured.

Perfect, I thought, rushing across the room to an empty chair in the back.

"Mr. Sinclair, this is your last warning. My hands are tied," a teacher snapped. He was tall, bald, and imposing.

"I'm *so* sorry, I promise it won't happen again... sir." The student—Jonathan—drawled.

This was closer to the boy I knew.

"You may call me Mr. Hale. Find your seat."

"Sorry, *Mr.* Hale," Jonathan blurted, turning to the rest of the class with a grin as he plopped into the seat next to mine.

This could not be happening.

Mr. Hale scowled before turning back to the board. "Like I was saying, open your textbooks to page 79, and read paragraph one through six. The author talks briefly about Emerald's hypo-pharmaceutical methods, and how this new technology may or may not be..."

"Hey, you. Emily?"

My eyes snapped off the page, flickering to Jonathan, now leaning across the small space between our desks.

"Yeah?" I whispered, struggling to focus on the words in front of me.

"Do you have an extra pen?"

"Oh, yeah," I mumbled, handing one to him with a faint smile. Jonathan smiled back, but when I turned back to my textbook, I could still feel his eyes on me.

"I used to know someone named Emily," he murmured, glancing up at me from the corner of his eye. "She was a bitch."

"Oh?"

"I'm sure you won't—"

"Talking is *not* permitted in my class," Mr. Hale glared, chalk raised accusingly towards Jonathan and me.

"Sorry," I squeaked, mentally cursing myself for even acknowledging Jonathan at all.

Another glare and silence fell back across the room as I tried and failed to keep my eyes glued to the page.

"You know, you look a lot like her."

"Really?" I whispered, knowing I should stay silent, but...

"Yeah," he murmured, scooting closer so we were almost face to face. "So sorry if I seemed a bit... unfriendly when we met."

"Oh. Yeah, okay," I whispered back, "I totally get it."

"Great," Jonathan said, smiling. "Thanks for the pen by the—"

"That's it, Miss Turner, Mr. Sinclair. Another peep out of you and detention!"

"She was just—"

"De-ten-tion."

Jonathan sighed, eyes rolling as he scooted back to his desk. Other students giggled quietly, until the teacher shot them a look.

"That's what I thought," Mr. Hale growled, turning back to the board.

I melted against my desk, cheeks reddening as I tried to apologize without words. Jonathan nodded, but his smile didn't quite reach his eyes. A chill crept down my spine, and for the rest of the class, I couldn't help but steal glances at him.

"EMILY!"

"Yeah?" I murmured, trying to shake the haze surrounding me since Science. I *was* glad I had found Clara by my locker, though.

"Did you hear anything I just said?" she asked, her eyebrows arched. I felt my cheeks warm slightly as I attempted a smile.

"Sorry."

Clara rolled her eyes, although her lips curled into a smile as well. "That's fine. Like I was saying, since you're new and all, I thought it might help if I came over to your house. To help you get adjusted and everything?"

"My house?" I said. "Today?"

"If that's good with you?"

"Yeah, yeah, yeah," I stammered. "Totally fine."

"Okay, great," Clara said, leaning back against her locker as she grabbed a silver phone. "Here."

I stood still, my brain taking a few moments to recognize her request.

"Right, sure," I said, fumbling with the combination lock as I tried in vain to twist through the numbers for the familiar click. My locker swung open, and piles of textbooks spilled over onto the floor. My face flushed as I tried in vain to scoop up the scattered books and papers.

"Mase, she's fine—"

"Chill, Clara. I don't mind," a deep voice responded as I looked up at Mason. He smiled casually, crouching down and easily gathering the books into a neat pile.

"Uh—thanks," I said, face flaming as I slid my books back into the dusty locker.

"Any luck finding your classes?"

"Is it that obvious?" I whispered, wincing at his soft laugh.

"Don't worry," he smiled. "We've all been through the same thing. Remember freshman year?"

"That was terrible," Clara said, giggling. "You were clueless."

Mason laughed again, his face lighting up as he turned back to me.

"Sorry I can't stay for long, but I didn't really get the chance to say: Welcome to Westview high school," he said with a grin, shooting Clara a playful look. "Hope it isn't *too* terrible here."

"Right. Thanks," I murmured as Mason walked away. I didn't understand how someone like him could be friends with someone like Jonathan. Saying they were polar opposites was an understatement.

"Emily? Hello?"

"Sorry," I said, turning back to Clara. I hadn't had many friends back in L.A. and wasn't the best at conversation. "You were saying?"

Clara sighed, pointing at the ancient flip-top phone in my hand. I was probably the only sixteen year old in the world who didn't own a smartphone.

"Your number?"

"Oh, sorry," I mumbled.

"Don't worry about it," Clara replied. Miraculously, she didn't seem to care about my phone. That *was* a first. "Also, you dropped something."

"What?"

"On the ground."

Oh, I thought, picking a crumpled piece of paper off the floor. I unfolded it absentmindedly, but froze as soon as I read the sentence scrawled there.

"We should get to class," I blurted, stuffing the note in my pocket as I steered Clara in the opposite direction.

"Okay," she puzzled. "See you later?"

“Of course.”

As soon as Clara was gone, I grabbed the note and slipped into the nearest empty room, the girl’s bathroom. I stared at the words, and couldn’t believe what I was reading.

`Did you really think I wouldn't recognize you?`

3
BEFORE

And here I had let myself forget about Jonathan. Tried to ignore that he was intertwined with *everything*.

What if he told everyone? What if I was thrown in jail? How could I—

But hey, I'm getting ahead of myself. I should start at the beginning, two years ago, back when I first met Jonathan. Besides, what better way to describe something than through a flashback. Little did I know what I was getting into.

~

ANY REGULAR FOURTEEN-GOING-ON-FIFTEEN year old would be nervous about their first day at a "new school." But I didn't give a single shit. Same thing would happen as it did the past three years, stupid connections and emotions. I—

"Emily, we're here."

"I can see that," I muttered, ignoring Mom's concerned face as I grabbed my backpack. She looked like any suburban Mom, old jeans, colorful tee, bright hair, minus the money though. I was surprised we still had *any* of that.

"Have a good day at school," she said with a smile.

I exhaled sharply, fixing her with a stare.

"Well... I love you," she responded as I slid out of the car. "Emily!"

"Love you," I grumbled, starting off towards my first high school, without a look back. Today definitely wasn't going to be good.

"WHAT THE HELL?" I shouted, staring at the scene before me in disgust. A tall, black-haired boy was grinning down at a thin, gangly one, splayed across the ground helplessly. I *hated* bullies. I would never stand by while something like this happened.

The black-haired boy glanced up at me, a glimmer shining in his dark eyes.

"I haven't seen you around her before," the boy spat, smiling in a way that made my toes curl.

"What gives you the right to do that?" I responded, almost regretting the way his face clouded in anger.

"And what gives you the right to talk to me when Kyle here," he glanced back at the scrawny kid, "asked for it?"

"I don't give a shit what Kyle did," I spat. "All I know is that you are a bully and a coward."

He glowered, walking right up to me, and once again, I was glad I could look him in the eye.

"You little—"

"Whoa whoa whoa," a second voice interjected, another boy pushing himself in-between us. He was taller than me, golden hair sweeping across his face as he shot me a look.

"I am *not* going anywhere," I muttered to him.

"Peter, chill. Our friend here's new, so she doesn't know how thing's work yet," he said, forcing me back slightly.

"Oh, really? She's seems to be fitting in fine." The black-haired boy, Peter, snapped, annoyance flashing across his face.

"She's nobody important," the blonde replied, a grin gracing his features.

"I swear to god, Sinclair—"

"We should get to class," the blonde said, right as the loud ringing of the bell echoed through the halls. Peter rolled his eyes, flipping around, but Kyle was gone, and by the time Peter turned, the blonde and I were as well.

We separated at the next turn, mouthed thank you's and haphazard glances the last thing we exchanged. For the rest of the day, I couldn't get him out of my mind. The mysterious boy who had stood up to Peter just the way I had. He seemed... different? Hopefully in a good way.

"You're not here to make friends," I reminded myself, entering my next class.

It flew by almost too quickly, as did the rest of the day. Three periods left. Two. One.

All the while, I repeated my thoughts like a mantra, knowing I couldn't form connections. Especially here.

And by the time I convinced myself I didn't want to see him, he appeared. I knew I should've left, or at least tried to evade detection, but as soon as he saw me, I couldn't stop myself from walking over. I didn't really care anyway.

"Hello, mystery man."

"Hey," he replied, a slightly-strange smile lighting up his face. "And you are?"

"Emily Turner, but you can call me Em."

"Jonathan," he said with a smirk.

"No nicknames?"

"No nicknames."

"Alrighty then, *Jonathan,* since I'm new, and you seem to be one of the only decent people in this school—" he nodded, eyebrows raising, "—it'd only be proper for us to be friends," I finished, leaning so we were face to face, less than a couple inches apart.

"With pleasure," Jonathan said, unflinching.

I smiled, leaning back and surveying him in a new light. He really was different.

"We should get to class," Jonathan murmured, offering his hand jokingly. We linked arms anyway, a warm feeling blossoming in my chest. Maybe making friends wouldn't be the worst possible situation. Maybe my first day at *this* school wasn't going to be too terrible.

4

AFTER

"Oh my god oh my god oh my god oh my—" I whispered, cutting myself off as I heard the door open.

Damn it.

I stuffed the note back into my pocket, avoiding the strange looks from the other girls as I practically ran out of the bathroom. Several minutes later, alongside checks of Clara's texts, I was at my next class.

Sighing in relief, I slipped into the seat farthest from the front, glad no one I knew was there. Hopefully I could actually pay attention to *this* class.

The rest of the day flew by, but I was still grateful I made it out of that classroom unnoticed. With a peek around the corner, I grabbed my backpack and was outside in minutes, glancing to confirm Jonathan was nowhere in sight.

I walked quickly to the front doors, wincing as cold air buffeted my hair and clothes. I scanned the parking lot, increasing to a run when I saw Mom's black sedan.

"How was your first day?"

"Fine," I lied.

"That's amazing!" she said, as if she actually believed me.

Sometimes it was hard to take in all of Mom. She was an optimistic extrovert, and with her bright hair and full frame, some people wondered if we were related at all. I was tall and thin, and with my natural light hair (before I dyed it), I assumed I looked more like my dad. When I was younger, I often asked about him, but eventually realized it'd be better to keep him on the torn-out side of pictures.

"I have to get back to work soon, but I might be back by dinner."

"Okay," I responded. She was always busy no matter where we lived.

"How do you like—"

She said this right when my phone buzzed.

"Mom?"

"Yeah?"

"A girl named Clara's coming over to help me adjust with school, if that's alright?"

Please say no.

"Really?!" she exclaimed, her face lighting up. "Honey, that's great! I told you changing things up would be good for you."

"Like we haven't changed things up enough," I murmured, regretting the words almost instantly.

"Emily..." she said softly.

"You should keep your eyes on the road."

A sigh.

"I'm sorry we've moved so much," Mom began. "You know I'd prefer not to, but ever since..."

"It's fine."

"Em—"

"We don't have to talk about this."

"Okay. If that's what you want."

I didn't respond. Silence ticked on, and surprisingly, Mom kept quiet. Another buzz from the flip-top broke it.

"Clara's on her way. Texting her the address now."

"All right," Mom said, tires screeching on gravel as we slid to a halt. "Since I'm probably not going to be home until nine, can you make sure your friend gets a ride home?"

A friend. "Yeah," I mumbled, getting out of the car. "I can also —" but she was gone, leaving me in front of the house we had lived in for five days. *Perfect.*

Seconds later I was inside, dropping my backpack on the ground and stepping out of my shoes.

My new home was small and weirdly claustrophobic, but felt more like a place I would live in as I saw the clothing bomb Mom had unleashed. She really did like to unpack.

I clenched my jaw, the walls around me seeming to collapse as tears stung the corners of my eyes. But I couldn't cry now. Clara would be here any minute.

And just like that, the doorbell rang. I cursed, dropping my backpack by the kitchen table and scrubbing tears away as I pulled the door open.

"Hey..."

"Hi!" Clara said cheerfully, waving goodbye to a silver car as she pushed past me into the house.

"Wow, your house is so cute!" Clara exclaimed. "I mean, it's so... cozy. Where's your room?"

"Down the hall," I said, the note burning a metaphorical hole in my pocket.

With a bounce, Clara disappeared into my room, and knowing

she wouldn't stay there for long, I slipped the note into a trashcan before joining her.

"You should really decorate more in here."

"Probably," I mumbled, giving my room a second look. It consisted mostly of a bed, a pile of clothes, and stacks of half-empty boxes.

"This is nice," Clara said, pointing out the one personal item in my room: an old photo. "Is this you?"

"Yeah," I replied, resisting the urge to push her away. It was mostly a reminder to Mom that I wasn't a complete zombie. I still had *some* semblance of emotions. *If only she knew.*

"Where is this... L.A.? You were blonde, right? Yeah, that's what I thought. But brown looks good, too, makes your eyes pop, y'know? Anyways, did you decide to change it there or was this a post-breakup thing? You know I did the same thing a while ago..." Clara babbled, her words struggling to take root in my mind. In one side and out the other.

"Emily?"

"Yep. Sweaty and blonde. Happy to move," I said harshly, regretting the way it made Clara flinch.

"Okay," she murmured, "we should probably start working soon."

"Agreed," I said, joining Clara's new position on my bed. "What'd you have in mind?"

"Well," Clara said, pulling out a binder. "There's a bunch of things actually, especially with the Emerald Project Ms. Miranda assigned, so I was thinking we could just go over that?"

"Sounds good."

"Before we begin, though," Clara paused, a blush creeping up her cheeks. "There's been something on my mind."

"Oh?"

"If you don't mind, of course."

"Sure," I said, even though I wasn't sure at all.

"So... there's this guy."

"Okay," I mumbled, resisting the urge to grimace as Clara leaned closer. I *really* wasn't a physical person.

"You met him today, actually."

My heart dropped.

"I have a feeling you and Nate are gonna be great friends," Clara said with a giggle, "and, well, if you could put in a good word for me."

"Really?"

"Really really." She blushed more, looking up at me hopefully.

"You know, Clara, I'm not sure if Jonathan is the one you want."

She frowned. "What?"

"Um..." *Damn it. You've really backed yourself into a corner here.*

"Nate's amazing. He's funny, smart, cool, kind. Was *really* nice to you, what else could you want?"

"Heh." I smiled wide. "Don't know what I was thinking."

"So... will you talk to him for me?"

"Sure."

"Perfect! Thanks, Emily—trust me, you won't regret it."

"Uh huh...Will you be ready if I take a quick stop at the bathroom?"

She nodded, features smiling again as I hastily left the room. In the bathroom, I ran the sink, splashing myself with the cold water.

Of course Clara was caught up in everything. Yet again, I'd managed to screw up the one normal thing in my life. I exhaled, this type of thinking was the opposite of helpful. I took a moment, focused, then headed back to my room.

What I didn't expect was the stab of fear when I saw what

Clara was doing. She grabbed something from underneath my bed, something I *definitely* didn't want her seeing.

"What are you doing?" I shrieked, rushing to her side and kicking the overflowing crate across the room.

Clara turned, eyes wide and guilty. "I—I didn't mean to—"

"What the hell?"

5

AFTER

"I—I'm sorry," Clara said. "I dropped my pencil underneath your bed and it fell into the crate and then you came in and... I really didn't mean to."

Clara looked sincere, pencil gripped tightly in her hand, staring at me with scared eyes.

"It's... fine," I mumbled, pushing the crate farther into the corner. "I just overreacted."

"No, you didn't," Clara said, standing and walking towards me. "Whatever you wrote in those journals was obviously private, and I intruded."

"Yeah," I murmured, glancing back over at the overflowing crate. They were overused and old, filled to the pages with emotions and secrets. I didn't want someone I had just met reading them. Especially since *everything* from last year was there, and if the person reading them had a thing for Jonathan... bad. Very bad.

"I'm really sorry," she said, pulling me into a hug. Unexpectedly, I returned it, the panic fading as I realized just how earnest Clara was. She wasn't lying.

"Don't worry about it," I said, sighing. "We should get back to work, though."

"Definitely," Clara said, releasing me with a big grin on her face. "Okay, back to the project."

I smiled, it'd been a long time since I'd seen someone so happy doing homework. I joined her on the bed again, and throughout the next couple hours, I forgot about Jonathan, my piles of journals, my problems, all my everything. It was incredible. Amazing. Temporary.

After Clara left, I felt empty, like her presence was the only thing keeping me from freaking out about everything.

It was late, nearly 11, when I finally heard the door open. I waited several minutes, sliding to my feet as I slipped back into the kitchen.

A minute later, I was back in my room, head pounding as I pulled the crate of journals back from their hiding place under my bed. I slipped the note into the newest one, my fingers twitching with the want to fill its pages. And yet, I knew I couldn't.

Journaling for me was like crack for others. Dangerously deadly. An addiction.

I slammed the journal shut, pushing the crate back underneath my bed as I plunged the room into darkness. I didn't sleep much that night.

THE NEXT MORNING everything seemed to pass in a confused daze, like my head was wrapped in a thick layer of gauze, preventing me from thinking clearly. I was at school within the hour, and classes passed the same way as yesterday. Slow and painful.

And yet, everything inside was quick and chaotic. Scratches and ink and... relief?

"Miss Turner?"

My head snapped up, meeting the gaze of a tall, pale woman. Her eyes narrowed, pinched face crinkling as she glared at me.

"This class ended five minutes ago."

"I'm sorry," I muttered, scooping my textbooks as quick as I could.

"I'm afraid I'll have to—" she paused, squinting down at me. "Who is Peter Lockman?"

"What?!" I gulped, clutching my textbooks tighter as I stumbled backward. *How did she know that name?*

"Mrs. Davis?" A smooth voice called from behind me.

Jonathan slouched by the door, face surprised and light, head tilting slightly to the side.

"Yes?"

"I was sent to come find Emily," he replied, eyes flickering to mine, a smirk curling on his lips.

Liar. He knew. It didn't make sense for anyone else to write that note.

"Miss Turner can leave as soon as she explains what she did to her textbook," Mrs. Davis snapped, her pinched face turning back to mine. "Textbooks aren't cheap, and we can't have students *defacing* them."

"I didn't do anything to my textbook," I whispered, jaw clenching as I shoved the textbook onto the table.

"I don't tolerate lying," Mrs. Davis said, long hands flicking open my textbook. "What is this?"

The entire inside cover was heavy with ink. Numbers, symbols, diagrams, words, random phrases, but most importantly, the words "Peter Lockman" were scrawled in the center, dark.

"What?"

"This is your textbook, yes?"

"Yeah," I murmured, my fingers trailing over the harshly

scratched names. I stopped when I saw the dark ink stains on my hands. I didn't remember doing this, I didn't even remember thinking about Peter in years, but somehow...

"Who is Peter Lockman?" Jonathan's voice cooed from behind me.

You know exactly who Peter Lockman is! I thought, anger thrashing inside me, the empty classroom losing its color.

"Miss Turner?" Mrs. Davis said, her eyes narrowing even further when I stayed silent.

"Emily?" Jonathan said, his face furrowed with concern, contrasting the cruel laughter in his eyes.

"I didn't want it to come to this," Mrs. Davis began, "but I think I'll need to talk to the principal. Your mother, too, I expect."

And *that* was the last straw.

"Do you honestly think I care about your stupid textbooks? And by the way, my family and I are completely fine without your help!"

I grabbed my textbook, ripped out the offending page and wadded it into a ball that I tossed to the ground. Then I stormed past them both, glaring.

At this point, I didn't give a shit what either of them thought.

~

For the rest of the day, each class flashed by in a mindless blur, similar to the strange haze I was feeling that morning. And yet, this kind of silence had one thing that differed from the haze. I was thinking. Overanalyzing. Worrying.

Why would Jonathan send me that note?

What did he want from me?

How was I supposed to keep this a **secret?**

~

THE REST of the week passed without disturbance, but everything was definitely not fine. Those thoughts spiraled downwards, becoming more and more time-consuming until it felt like my head was going to explode.

Jonathan became strangely absent as well, sometimes disappearing for hours at a time, which to me was more of a bad thing than a good one. Since the note, I had heard nothing from him, which seemed infinitely worse than if he had continued to taunt me. Jonathan knew more than I did, and that knowledge made the week like Hell.

And still, the highlight was Clara. She was almost always positive and helped lessen the heavy weight crushing my shoulders, even though it was difficult to be happy when I was lying to her all the time. Ever since we had exchanged numbers, we texted almost every day. It made me feel nicer, despite the circumstances.

Things seemed to be going uphill from there, but the dark feeling in my mind wouldn't vanish, and sooner or later, I'd know why.

6

AFTER

"Emily?"

I could tell by the tone in Mom's voice something wasn't right.

"Coming," I yelled back, shutting my textbook and wincing at the remains of the page I had ripped out. I was pretty sure I knew what was going on. But as the textbook closed and I glimpsed the remnants of my frenzied writing left printed on the next page, doubt flashed through me.

I knew Mom was busy enough as it was, especially being home before nine on a Saturday, and I definitely didn't need to add to that.

I slid to my feet, a soft buzz stopping me in my tracks. I felt a smile twitch across my face as I picked up the flip-top vibrating amongst the piles of textbooks cluttered on my bed. Clara's texts always cheered me up. I opened it with a click, the cracked screen lighting up with a text from a number I didn't know.

I need a favor.

The smile melted off my face, a blank feeling of resignation flying through me. I should've expected Jonathan would contact me eventually.

`Who are you?`

I wrote anyway, listening to my gut.

"Emily!" Mom's voice shouted, not angry yet, just strained.

"Sorry," I responded, hitting the send button as I slipped the flip-top into my pocket.

Stay cool, I thought, *everything's fine.*

I walked down the pale-pink walls into the largest room in the house. Mom sat by the table that took up most of the room, palms pressing hard against her temple, shoulders loose and desolate. She looked like she had given up.

"Mom?" I whispered, gently sitting down opposite her. She sighed heavily, the dark circles under her eyes impossible to ignore.

"I got an email from the principal today," she said quietly. Guilt hit me like a train, and at that moment, all I wanted to do was curl up in a corner and hide.

"They said something about an outburst?" Mom continued, "and doing something to your textbook?"

My eyes flickered to the ground, unable to meet her tired eyes.

"Now, I'm not mad, but... I thought... we all thought you were..." she exhaled, her words faltering.

'We all thought you were doing better.'

"Mom," I whispered, looking up earnestly into her face, "I don't know what happened. I'm so sorry, I thought everything was better, too. I don't know how to... I mean it just..."

"They said we'd have to pay for the textbook, and you'll have to stay after school in detention for a week."

"Okay."

"I just wish you could tell me what's wrong..." Mom muttered, more to herself than to me.

"Nothing's wrong," I said quietly. "You don't have to worry, it won't happen again."

Mom smiled faintly, looking at me in the way that only mothers can.

"I hope so," she said, shaking her head as she rose to her feet. "I think I'm going to get some sleep, I have an early shift tomorrow."

"Okay," I murmured, hoping I had convinced her everything was fine. Because, truly, I didn't know what I felt at the moment.

She smiled half-heartedly, covering a yawn with her hand as she disappeared into her room. I smiled back, but as soon as I was sure she couldn't see me, my face turned blank. I stumbled to my room, fatigued body and brain urging me to succumb to sleep. But the buzz in my back pocket jerked me back to reality.

You know who I am.
And you know what I can do.

Do I?

I typed quickly, worry knotting into my stomach as the dark force stirred. Delivered. Read at 12:49.

You do. Don't deny it.
Stalling won't prevent anything.

What do you want?

You know exactly what I want, a favor.

What makes you so sure I'll do something?

My hands were shaking now.

You don't want anyone to know about Peter.

Don't talk about him.

The next words could potentially change everything. It all depends on the phrasing.

I won't do anything for you, I typed, deleting the words quickly. I couldn't let denial control this conversation.

Are you blackmailing me?! Deleted. I couldn't let anger control the situation either.

"Uhhhh." I fell back against my pillows and piles of textbooks, harsh blue light illuminating the rest of my untouched room.

The gentle buzz warming my leg brought me back.

Don't hide from me.

Short sentences, maybe four, five words, packed as much punch as elaborate paragraphs. Everything with Jonathan wasn't always quick and simple.

I'm not hiding.
Just thinking.

There isn't much to think about. I know what I want, I'm certain you know what to do. What you need to do.
And yet the question is, will she pick the right

answer? Will she even pick the answer to the right question?

More words. He was getting angry.

The answer is obvious.

A lot of things are obvious, and this sure wasn't obvious. What the hell did Jonathan want?

I won't wait any longer.
Choose.

The world seemed to leech of color. Then suddenly, I understood. A choice had to be made that I should've realized in the beginning. The only thing that was would keep everything secure inside and out.

Time's up.

I had to do this, for Mom, and Clara, and even Mason. I couldn't let Jonathan win, but I couldn't stand back and let my life get ruined.

Wait.
I'll do it.

7

BEFORE

It had been two weeks since I'd met Jonathan, and at first, everything had been perfect. We'd become thick as thieves, always together, always on the edge of *something*. I didn't know what we were to each other, and I didn't really want to.

But then something happened.

~

"He did what?" I said, dragging Jonathan across the room to an almost empty hall.

He laughed, leaving his lunch tray on our table, smiling big.

"*Peter Lockman* actually invited you to his party?"

"Crazy, I know," Jonathan whispered, pulling me closer, "and there's nothing against plus ones."

"Me and you," I scoffed, "at Peter's party?"

"Where else?"

"Drunk idiots and topless freshman. Funnnnn."

Jonathan rolled his eyes, but they sparkled as he found me again. "I wouldn't mind seeing you topless."

"Uh huh," I snapped, pushing him away. "In your dreams."

"How did you know?!" he exclaimed.

I tried to frown, but couldn't stop the laugh from leaking out. "Okay, fine. But why do you want to go anyway?"

"What else am I supposed to do?"

He had a point, but...

"With Peter?"

"He's not actually that bad," he said slowly.

"Seriously?"

I frowned at his nod. Jonathan usually hated Peter. He was a special sort of terrible.

"See you tonight?"

"Jonathan Sinclair, on a school night?!"

"Gotta prepare for college somehow."

We both smiled, the strange feeling fading. "I'll think about it."

"I'll pick you up at eight," he said with a wink.

"If you're lucky!" I called after him. He didn't look back.

I glanced at my flip-top, a new but old gift from Mom before we moved. It was 12:57, which gave me about seven hours. Seven hours to perfect my plan.

"You look good," Jonathan said, bringing a slight flush to my cheeks.

"Thanks," I murmured, resisting the urge to cross my arms. I was wearing one of Mom's old dresses, minimal frills and a deep blue."You don't look so bad yourself."

"Well?" he said, grinning as he opened the passenger door with a flourish. "Ladies first."

"Why, thank you," I said, walking past him to the large oak door. A quick ring of the bell and we were in.

More people showed than I'd thought. Sickly-sweet aromas hung in the air, and people clustered around the room as music throbbed in the background. Almost everyone had a plastic cup.

"If you don't mind," Jonathan said, disappearing into the crowd with a salute.

Okay, I thought, smiling more for show than anything. *Perfect. Cause* I *know exactly what to do.*

EVENTUALLY I'D MADE my way over to the keg in the corner of the room, and several cups later everything was a bit more interesting. Little did I know my night was just beginning.

"Heyyyy Em," a voice said as something heavy draped over my shoulder.

"Hey," I cooed, stopping when I saw the unfamiliar face behind me. The boy was short and stocky, eyes squinty and red as they lingered on me uncomfortably. "Who are you?"

"Does it matter?" he garbled, hand beginning to move.

"Get off of me," I barked, shaking his arm off my shoulder. But as soon as I did, his other arm curled around my waist. "Get off of me!"

"Shhh," he whispered, the putrid smell of weed clinging to him heavily. I struggled against him, but the world was much too slow and out of focus for it to do much good. Fear stabbed me as he moved closer, my scream cut short as I was knocked to the ground.

"She said get off," someone yelled from the crowd forming around us. I stumbled to my feet, trying to focus on the two grappling boys on the ground. One was high, one was blonde. I knew a blonde... right?

"Jonathan?"

A grunt from Jonathan as he slammed the other boy face first into the floor. *Yep.* I leaned closer, feeling inexplicably drawn to the fight. It was a dance of fists and blood, something wrong but something I couldn't take my eyes away from.

"Hey, hey!" another boy shouted, someone I recognized quickly as Peter. He jumped between them. "Stop it, stop. Kurt!" he growled, shoving the short boy back.

"For shit's sake," he snapped, turning to me with a red face. "Why are *you* here?"

"Long story," I said, giggling. His eyes narrowed, walking straight up to me. I only giggled harder. Damn booze.

"Emily, right." It wasn't really a question.

"Uh-huh."

"Get out."

"Uh-huh."

His face blazed, a hard pressure snapping against my arm. This time I was prepared. A slap, and Peter stumbled back, honest-to-god shock on his face.

"Oops," I whispered.

"What the hell—" Peter spat, shooting Jonathan a deadly look, "—was that?"

Jonathan shrugged, and I laughed at the slight smile.

"I—"

"They're here!" a voice shouted from the crowd. "COPS OUTSIDE!"

All. Hell. Broke. Loose.

It's difficult to remember exactly what happened after that. What I do remember is shrieks, frenzied breath, and groups of teenagers streaking into the pitch-black night. Everything was blurry and surreal.

~

The next day was miserable. My head hurt and it seemed like I would never be able to drink enough water; I don't know how I would've survived a school day. Mom must've known something was wrong, but to her credit, she never asked.

After she turned in for the night, I laid on my own bed, thinking about the party, Jonathan, and the fight, when there was a knock on the door. It was 1:38. In the morning. Someone was about to get an earful.

I opened the door with a yawn, letting out a quiet shriek as someone fell onto me.

"Jonathan?

He lifted his head: black, blue, and dazed.

"Hey Em," he murmured, "I might have a little problem."

PART 2

8

AFTER

You have a plan, I kept telling myself throughout the grueling process of the next day. Sunday was meant to be relaxing, a time to hang out with friends, or catch up on homework. For me, the minutes ticked by like hours. I didn't seem to have the attention to focus on anything for more than a few minutes.

I sat in my room for most of the day, constantly checking the cracked screen of the flip-top or staring into space. I couldn't study, couldn't relax, not with the new information swirling around in my head. That knowledge was like a dark force that plagued me day and night. Cold and clawing and unbeatable.

Tap tap tap. Click click click click. Tap tap tap. My fingers drummed on my knees, a rhythmic sound that helped pass time as minutes marched by. The flip-top lay by my side as I checked its dark screen constantly to confirm nothing had changed.

My head lay against the dashboard of my bed, eyes closed, words rewritten across my eyelids from the night before. Why was he taking so long?

Time's up.

I'll do it.

Centralwood Avenue, 12 am.

Jonathan hadn't texted me after that, and as the unknown deadline drew closer, anxiety threatened to overwhelm me.

Tap tap tap. Click click click click. Tap tap tap.

Eight hours.

Seven.

Six.

Sky darkened. Stars beginning to break through the grey, polluted sky. They were hiding the way I should.

Five.

Four.

The creak of the front door as Mom tried to sneak in without a sound. Little did she know I was still awake, wide-eyed and staring into darkness. The more time crept by, the more the anticipation grew and the faster my fingers drummed against my knees, the floor, my desk.

Tap tap tap. Click click click click. Tap tap tap.

Two hours left. One. Half an hour.

I slid out of my bed, wincing at the soft thump as my feet hit the floor. I crept through my room and minutes later I was wrapped in a thick black coat, with dark leggings and boots to match. I let my hair down over my face as well. Unrecognizable.

Now for the dangerous part. I approached the front door, flinching at the loud creak. I froze, the sound of slow footsteps echoing through the house. I stepped back into the shadow of the door, holding my breath as I inched it closed.

Mom's form staggered into the kitchen, her eyes glazed and hair tangled. She stumbled to the sink, the sound of rushing water echoing around the room.

My back pressed hard against the wall as adrenaline pumped through my veins, ears straining as I tried to pinpoint where she was. The faucet switched off, the clatter of a cup hitting the floor as a mumbled curse echoed from near the table.

I pressed farther into the shadows, waiting until I heard Mom's soft footsteps retreating into her room. I slid to my feet, checking once behind my shoulder as I nudged the door open and disappeared into the cool night air.

THE NIGHT SKY was no longer a grey, but now an inky black that seemed to swallow up the stars. Cold air buffeted against my clothing, hair whipping around my face as I tried to discern where I was. Everything looked drastically different in the dark, the trees and houses and cars menacing in a way they would've never been in daylight.

Get it together, I thought, pulling my dark clothes tighter against my body. A shuffle and the flip-top illuminated everything around me as I Googled where Jonathan told me to go. Conveniently, it was only a twenty minute walk away.

I checked the flip-top again, before slipping it back into my pocket as I jogged into the darkness. Fear fueled me to run faster and faster, knowing the closer I got to Jonathan, the farther I was from doing the right thing. But was there even a right thing? This was my only choice... right?

I had promised Mom only a day before that I was getting

better, and this really seemed like a step in the opposite direction. But I kept running. I didn't stop until I saw the pale green sign: *Centralwood Avenue.*

It was so quiet that my labored breathing was the only sound... at least until the flip-top vibrated.

Have you arrived?

I'm here.

As soon as I hit send, something creaked in the dark woods behind me. I whipped around, scanning the trees until a dark figure stepped out.

I wobbled backwards, hands reaching for a weapon that wasn't there. I was so afraid I couldn't even scream. Eventually the figure stopped before me and pulled back a black hood.

I would recognize that face anywhere.

Jonathan sneered at me, his features twisting grimly, and I knew he enjoyed how afraid I was.

"I knew you'd come."

"What choice did I have?"

Jonathan reached inside his pocket and pulled a scrappily wrapped parcel into the dim light. His light hair almost shone in the moonlight, and someone could've almost called him beautiful in that moment of distraction. But as his face turned back to mine, the moment was ruined, along with my wistful thinking. Jonathan wasn't the same boy anymore.

"Here."

I stepped forward cautiously, taking the parcel from his open hands. "What do you want me to do?"

Jonathan's eyes narrowed but the smile remained.

"I want you to take this," he said, gesturing at the parcel, "and keep it for me. I'll tell you when I want it back."

"That's it?" I said, eyes glancing to the small, baseball-sized parcel in my hands.

"You sound disappointed," he muttered, eyebrows curving upward delicately. "Expecting something... different?"

"No," I responded. "Is this everything?"

He smiled again, white teeth seeming to glow in the darkness. "Yes. Except there's one rule: Don't even think about opening it."

"Why?"

"Did I ask for questions?"

Fire fluttered deep in my stomach, but dread and loathing snuffed it out just as quick. Jonathan's piercing eyes were the last thing I saw before he pulled the hood back over his face.

"Don't open it."

I nodded.

Satisfied, he turned around, footsteps strangely silent as he disappeared back into the woods.

I shivered, cold air and the dark night sky swirling around me. Inhaling deeply, my heart finally slowed as I turned back home. And yet, I would only realize by the time I stood before my front door, that as soon as Jonathan had left, the nighttime sounds returned to the woods.

9
AFTER

On the way home I wondered what Jonathan wanted me to do, but it was no use. All I knew was that I was in trouble, that the past I had tried so hard to forget was back, looming larger than ever.

The night was cold and my breath took on the shape of small, silver clouds that looked like... like...

SUDDENLY I WAS FALLING, endless blue spots twirling around me, blurring together into a shrill whine that became a pounding, blistering pain. A burn blazed in my chest, spreading outwards, consuming everything. The whine twisted, flipping the endless black into a crystal clear image. Lights. Flashing bright red, blue, white, yellow. Shouting, loud and urgent. Tainted with fear. People rushing around, whine turning into flashing sirens and a single scream.

I COLLAPSED AGAINST THE GRAVEL. Hard. It wasn't the first time this had happened, and after a couple of desperate Google searches I diagnosed myself with panic attacks. But honestly... they were so much more. They were flashbacks, the past rearing its head with a vengeance.

I scrubbed tears off my face and climbed to my feet. Running again. Running from my own memories. I would never escape them.

~

EVENTUALLY THE OUTLINE of my house appeared. Relief poured through me as I crept to the door. I wiped my face one last time, easing the door open, slight creaks disappearing into the familiar quiet. After a few moments, after no word from Mom, I decided she was asleep.

I stepped out of my boots, hanging the coat on the rack as I grabbed the flip top. It was 12:47. I sighed, it was too late to be up running errands in the night.

I crept back to my room, yawning as I shut the door with a click.

"Where the hell have you been?" a voice snapped behind me. "Do you have any idea what time it is?"

"I can explain," I whispered, gaze dropping to the ground.

"You better hope so," Mom said, her eyes welling with tears as she glared at me. "You don't know what it's like to wake up in the middle of the night and realize your daughter isn't there."

"I'm sorry," I mumbled, hands clasping and unclasping as I stood by my door.

"What were you thinking? Leaving without telling me?"

"I'm sorry Mom, I—"

Finally she stepped forward and took me into her arms.

"I'm so *so* angry with you," she said. "But I'm still so glad you're here." She pulled back, tears spilling down her cheeks. "Don't ever do that again."

"I won't."

"You better not or else you'll never leave this house again."

I hung my head, hugging Mom back as hard as I could. "I won't I won't I won't." Mom's emotions had always been volatile.

Her shoulders sagged, and she drew back, pulling me so we were both sitting on my bed. "Where did you go?"

I opened my mouth, wanting to tell her exactly where I'd been and why I'd been there, but I didn't. I couldn't.

"Is there something I should know about?" Her voice had gone cold, like I was a criminal suspect instead of her daughter. Which technically... she had every right to think that.

"I had a panic attack. I didn't want to wake you, so I went on a walk instead." I whispered. Half a truth, an improvement.

"Honey," she said. "I wish you'd tell me when things like this happen. Even though I work a lot, I still *need* to know when you have a panic attack." She pulled me closer, tight, tears flowing freely. "It *will* be okay. I promise. But I need you to talk to me, Em."

Her kinds words only made me cry harder. I was lying to protect her and she was still trying to help me. She still believed in me no matter what. It was incredible.

"You're still grounded, you know."

"I know," I sniffed. I wished we could stand like this forever. In the warmth and silence and peace of it all.

"It's past midnight," Mom whispered.

"I know," I mumbled back, a heavy exhaustion settling over me. "Just... a couple more min..."

She laughed then, and her humor calmed me more than a pill ever could. I drifted into her warmth, the dark force expelled from my mind if only for several hours. I didn't even dream that night. At least, I didn't remember the nightmares this time.

THE NEXT MORNING I woke up early, managing a couple bites of breakfast before rushing out the door. The car ride to school was unnaturally quiet. Mom acted like the previous night had never happened.

In a way, it seemed almost like last night *had* been a dream, a scared teen's imagination. But the messy package Jonathan had given me disproved that. For now, it was shoved under the bed, a predictable hiding place, but a hiding place nonetheless.

Mumbling a goodbye to Mom, I flew through my first classes, mind wandering to hundreds of different possibilities. Jonathan and I *did* meet last night, the parcel proved that, but was the midnight conversation with Mom more than just a thought? Could it be memory, or a need satisfied through my subconscious? I was stuck in my own world, thought no one could break me out of that strange state of mind, but again, I was wrong.

"Hey, Earth to Emily, Earth to Emily!?" Clara laughed, waving her hand in front of my face.

"Yeah, sorry," I blinked, attempting to focus.

"Mase just asked how your weekend was?"

"Mase?" I murmured slowly, Mason's dark-haired form popping into view beside me. He waved, a smile lighting up his face almost awkwardly.

"I hope I'm not intruding," he said, glancing back at Clara lightly. She shook her head, a laugh curling on her lips as I flushed.

"Oh... uh, sorry."

"Don't mention it," Mason said.

"My weekend was normal," I blurted, my face reddening even further. *Instant* regret.

"Normal?" Clara giggled, shooting Mason another look. "Well that sounds just wonderful."

He rolled his eyes.

"Hey, Mase!" Jonathan shouted, sliding to a halt beside us.

"Nate," Clara whispered, as if she didn't want him to hear.

"Mase, Clara," Jonathan said, nodding his head in acknowledgement before his eyes settled on mine.

"Em."

"Em?" Clara asked, surprised.

"It's Emily," I murmured.

"Emily, right," Jonathan purred, not-so-subtly winking in Clara's direction. "Why don't you tell us more about Saturday?" he continued.

Mason glanced back and forth between us, as if he was confused.

"What happens on Saturday?" he finally asked.

"Right, sorry," Clara said, giggling. "Basically, the Juniors throw a party every year. And well..." She stopped, looking back at Jonathan, eyes sparkling.

"We're invited," he finished with a smirk.

"A party?" I asked.

"Uh-huh," Clara said, all wide-eyes and smiles. "You're coming?"

"I certainly am," Jonathan replied. "Mase?"

"I'm in," he said.

"Em?"

"Sure..." I whispered, glaring at the floor.

"This is perfect!" Clara squealed. "What better way to initiate you to—"

"Mr. Sinclair? Miss Turner?"

It was Mr. Hale. He did not look pleased.

"I'm uncertain how you've avoided it for this long," he growled, "but both of you are due for detention this week."

"Of course," Jonathan said smoothly, slipping his arm through mine with a smile. "My apologies. We'll go now."

"Right," Mr. Hale grumbled. "Good. Miss Fallon, Mr. Taylor, off to class."

Mason nodded, waving slowly. He still looked extremely confused. He wasn't the only one.

"Don't forget about Saturday!" Clara shouted, as Jonathan dragged me away.

"Get off of me," I growled, knowing that, presumably, Jonathan and I would be alone for the next hour. *Perfect.*

"Doesn't this party sound fun?" he said in a stage whisper.

"Drop the act," I snapped. Jonathan knew, in terms of messing up, the last party we'd been to was hard to beat.

IO

BEFORE

"What are you doing here?" I whispered, dragging him inside. "And your face, what happened?"

Jonathan grimaced, wincing as he moved. He was one big puzzle piece of bruises, starting at his jaw and creeping under his shirt. "They're not all from today."

"Still," I said, pulling him into my room. "I'm being serious."

"I know," he murmured, sliding to the ground. "I mean... I —ugh."

"Spit it out."

"Em, there's something I haven't told you," he said with a deep sigh. "It's my sister."

"If you don't feel comfortable talking about this—"

"I want to tell you. It's just so difficult." He took a deep breath. "My sister, Lena, has schizophrenia. Aripiprazole, her medication, is *really* expensive... and our dad isn't around anymore. So it's just kinda me and her and..."

"Jonathan, I—" tears began to well in my eyes as I scooted next to him. He was cold, shaking slightly. "You didn't have to—"

"I'm not done," he said quietly. "There's this guy. He offered me a lot of money if I delivered certain substances for him. It's the only way I've been able to afford the meds. But last night, someone overdosed and..." He began to shake harder. "My employer didn't like it."

As soon as the words left Jonathan's lips, he was up, already crossing the room.

"Jonathan, wait."

"I shouldn't have told you anything."

"It's fine, actually, I—"

"This puts *everything* at risk," he shot back, turning to me with glistening eyes. "This was so *stupid.* I've known you for a week and—"

"Hey," I said, grabbing his sleeve. "It's okay."

"No, it's not. I can't—"

"Shut up."

He stopped, a small smile peaking through. "Can you stop interrupting me?"

"Shut up," I replied, plopping both of us onto the foot of my bed. "You're catastrophizing."

"Clearly."

"Look," I said. "It's not great what you've done. But telling me was the right thing. You could probably use some help to figure out what to do."

"Yeah," Jonathan said with a snort.

"What I'm trying to say is... don't worry. We *will* find a solution."

"We?"

"Of course," I said, smiling. "First of all, I swear whoever hit you is going to face some serious shit."

He turned, eyes darkening. "Don't try to find them, okay?"

"But how am I supposed to—"

"I'm serious."

"Okay," I said. "We'll find another way. But for now, let's clean you up."

"I can do it at home," Jonathan replied. "It's late anyway."

"Are you sure?"

"I'm okay."

"Okay."

"Thanks," he whispered, pulling me into a stiff hug.

"Besides," I said. "What's freshman year without some difficulties?"

He laughed. "Thank you, Em. You're... really amazing."

"Duh," I replied, smiling. "But you're right, it is two in the morning."

"I know, I know," he said, getting to his feet. "I'll go."

"See you tomorrow?"

"Definitely."

A smile and a wave, and Jonathan was gone.

~

I SIGHED, collapsing back onto my bed with a smile. I had genuinely helped somebody! That was something new and warm and fluttery and amazing. Jonathan was someone special. At least, that's what I thought.

In a daze, I flicked the light off, grabbed a drink of water and fell back into bed. I snuggled deep underneath the covers, and was almost asleep when I heard something strange.

"I told you not to call me tonight."

I jerked awake, straining to hear. It sounded like someone was just outside my window.

"I know, but I'm serious this time," the voice hissed. It was definitely coming through my open window, but it was hard to hear among the sound of wind and creaking branches.

"I can't tonight, okay? I know she's asleep."

They sounded close, really close. Someone was outside my bedroom window, in the middle of the night, talking about *me.*

"Lockman, I swear..."

Lockman. That name sounded agonizingly familiar. In fact, that voice did as well. It tugged on my consciousness, deliciously close enough to distract me from the phone call.

"I'm leaving. I don't care. Bye." Shuffling, and it was silent. They were gone.

I shivered, knowing I wouldn't fall asleep anytime soon.

II

AFTER

Detention was slow and painful, even worse than normal classes. We were supposed to write a paper on how we could have handled the situation differently, but Jonathan wouldn't shut up. I had three sentences written by the end of the hour.

The rest of the week was no different. Between the piles of homework, Jonathan's shameless flirting, Clara's prodding, Mason with all his... perfectness, and the absolute indecision with the parcel, it made my week a special kind of torture.

Jonathan's acting was perfect.

Every joke or wink or timed grin set me off. And Clara only made it worse. She had fallen hard, leaving Mason and me out of the picture. Today, Wednesday, I finally mustered the courage to ask him about it.

"Mase?"

"Yeah?" he said, dropping back so we were walking in line.

"Have you, I mean, um... sorry, I can't speak at all today." I exhaled. "Are you alright?"

“Me?” Mason said with a laugh. “Are *you* okay?”

“I’m fine.”

He stopped, letting Clara and Jonathan continue. “Did you know the average person says ‘I’m fine’ 14 times a week,” he paused, taking my hands gently. “Only 19% mean it. So, again, are you okay?”

“Yes.”

“You sure?”

“I’m sure,” I whispered, blush creeping up my cheeks. “Thanks.”

“Anytime,” he replied. “Let’s go?”

“Yeah,” I said, smiling back as we caught up.

Clara was beaming, practically bouncing with energy as she turned around. “Emily, okay, you have to—”

“One sec,” I interrupted, grabbing the buzzing flip-top in my pocket. “It’s probably just my Mo...”

It’s time.

“Really,” I whispered, glaring at Jonathan’s much-too-innocent face.

“What is it?” He asked.

“Emily, I need—”

“Crap. Sorry,” I muttered, trying to focus. “I really have to go. Sorry, Clara, I’ll call you later? Mase, Jonathan.”

“Bye!” Mason said, a strange look on his face.

“Thanks,” I called back, ignoring the urge to shudder as I slipped away. Jonathan really did have terrible timing.

I HAD COOLED off a bit by 8. Mom was gone, as usual, and I had the next couple hours to myself. It was dusk, light enough to see, but dark enough to have your headlights on. Dangerous.

I had grabbed the parcel, layering myself in dark, baggy clothing as I stepped outside. Hopefully, the parcel was hidden enough under my shirt. Hopefully... no one would notice the strangely dressed teen, a suspicious bulge under her coat.

"JONATHAN?" I whispered, heart pounding too loud as I peeked around a wall into the dark alley. Shadows hid the passageways, overturned trashcans and boxes piling over the dirty ground. It was dark now, definitely nighttime.

I clenched the parcel tighter, carefully picking my way through the trash. It had begun to rain, the cool downpour dripping down my coat and puddling around me. When I reached the address Jonathan had given me, it took all my courage not to turn and run.

Instead I took a deep breath, glancing once at the grey sky, before trying the rusty doorknob on the house in front of me. The door was old, steps leading up to it stained and mossy, while the house was small and painted dark, shingles faded and loose.

The door swung open, revealing a short hallway layered in shadows and dirt. I stepped inside, leaving wet footprints on the bare floor as I shut the door with a creak. I stayed silent, hands trembling as the sounds of life outside disappeared to a bone-chilling silence. I inched forward, eyes straining in the dark as I reached the end of the hallway.

A low arch opened to an equally small room, with an old, worn table and two chairs. Kitchen appliances were shoved up against the walls, everything covered in the sort of dust and grime you only see deposited by time's aging.

The lone light shone through an old window, boarded up and covered by a large sheet. I felt myself holding my breath and freezing in my tracks as I realized the way subtle portions of the floor were slightly discolored, small and round, almost like... footsteps.

Tensing, I flipped around, thoughts sinking lower and lower as I saw the outline of a human shadow cast across the room. Reaching for the parcel and turning slowly towards the exit, I crept forward, eyes zeroed in on the dark door.

"Stop. Turn around, and put the package on the table."

I flinched, grabbing the parcel with shaking hands as I faced the sharp voice. A dark figure walked out of the hallway, hooded and built differently from my blonde tormentor. Whoever standing before me wasn't Jonathan.

He was a short, small guy, dressed in a black hoodie and jeans, face hidden from view. He held one hand behind him while the other was shoved into his pocket. Despite his unassuming appearance, I couldn't stop shaking. I was in real danger here.

I walked forward, eyes never leaving the place where I knew his eyes would be, and placed the parcel on the table.

"Who are you?" His voice was low, garbled, and mechanical, like he was speaking through some kind of filter. Also, why would he be asking *me* who I was?

"Who the hell are you?" he shouted again, pulling the glinting shape of a gun from behind his back.

"Wait," I stammered, hands raising in front of me as I scrambled backwards. "My name is Emily."

"Why are you here?" he said, still pointing the gun at me. I was so afraid I could hardly remember how to form words.

"I was sent here by someone. Please don't hurt me, I don't even know—"

"What's in the package?"

"I—I don't know."

"God damn you, Sinclair," the figure muttered, the gun wavering slightly.

"Do you mean Jonathan? Yeah yeah, Jonathan sent me with this parcel thing and I don't even know what he wants me to do..."

I looked around the room for somewhere to go or something to defend myself with or—

"Please. Please don't kill me. My Mom—"

I fell to the ground, beginning to choke as tears ran down my face and panic made it impossible to breathe.

"Shut up," he snapped, moving to the table before inspecting the package. I made the tactical decision to keep my mouth shut tight. He swore, turning back to me quickly.

"Get up. Do you know why Sinclair sent you?"

I shook my head wildly. He sighed, grabbing the parcel with his free hand and slipping it inside his coat.

"Next time Sinclair makes you his errand boy, tell him it won't end nicely. I expect to *see* the people I rely on," the figure hissed, his gun never moving its position. "Not some fake," he continued, brushing a ginger curl off his face before disappearing out the door.

I laughed, collapsing to the ground, body shaking uncontrollably. The world swirled around me, bright colors and dull sounds, the icy floor pressing against my cheek a welcome cold.

What the hell had I gotten myself into?

~

I DIDN'T KNOW how long I spent on the floor, or how long it took to replace the thoughts or memories in my head. I even wondered if I should end it all. But when I did eventually get up, when I left that house and walked home, everything had changed.

I couldn't go back now. I was too deep into whatever corner of twisted secrets and favors Jonathan had forced me into.

This time I really *was* screwed.

12

AFTER

Everything was blank. Empty. Nonsensical. Then something flipped. Dark claws pulled me down into a restless sleep, plaguing me with screams and splashes.

I was stuck, trapped, put on display. Strong arms grabbed me, pushed me down, down, down.

Breath escaped my lungs in bubbles, now the only things I could see.

Eventually darkness came, snuffing out the burning in my chest. It didn't stop the pain, though. That was still unbearable.

I SHOT UPWARDS, hands tangled in sweat-soaked sheets as my room snapped into focus. I sighed, anger piercing through sleep's intoxicating haze.

Bright light illuminated my room, the pit in my stomach growing as I read the boxy numbers on the flip-top's screen. 2:58. Another night without sleep. Panic splashed into my stomach, and seconds later I was on the ground. A click and my room was plunged into darkness again, the familiar signs of insomnia beginning to show.

I stumbled out of my room, eyes throbbing as the tiled bathroom flooded with warmer light. I stared into the mirror hanging on the door, almost scared to meet the girl staring back at me.

Dark circles ringed her eyes, skin pale and hair a mess. A journal clenched tightly in her hand. The clicking of her pen a necessity.

I had stopped journaling months ago. It was like a drug, an addiction. Something to be pored over and analyzed and internalized minutes after the release that came from writing. But right now I needed that drug more than ever.

I wrote everything down. My new friendships, Clara, Jonathan, whatever I was feeling for Mason. Mom, how I felt about the last couple weeks, everything. Five pages later, the panic subsided. I sighed, sliding to the floor as exhaustion settled over me.

I didn't remember falling asleep, but the next thing I knew, light was shining into the bathroom and the faint sound of songbirds trilled outside. The smell of coffee wafted through the air, and everything seemed normal somehow. It was hard to accept after the night I'd had.

I hid my journal under the washing machine and went to find Mom, who was ready for work.

"Did you sleep in there?"

"My bed wasn't helping," I mumbled, ignoring her worried look as I pushed past and into my room.

"And sleeping in the bathroom solves that?" she said, voice muffled by distance as I searched for clothing that wasn't caked in mud or dust. "That's two nights in a row."

"I'm fine, Mom."

"Emily—"

"I don't want to be late."

~

"HEYYYYY EM, we're still up for Saturday, right?"

Resisting the urge to slam my locker, I turned to the nuisance beside me.

"Don't call me that."

"Ahhh," Jonathan said, "looks like someone didn't get her beauty sleep."

"Oh my god, Jonathan, will you just—" I paused. "We need to talk."

"Really?" Eyebrows arching and leaning against the lockers, he almost looked sincere. "Are you sure? Because with those dark circles, I don't think you should be talking to *anybody*."

"I'm serious."

"Well I'm serious about talking *later*," he responded, and for a second, I thought he might be telling the truth.

"Jonathan," I whispered, "that guy had a *gun*. I never would've—"

"Perfection. I'll see you on Saturday," he interrupted, focusing on something behind me.

I whipped around, the sight of Clara more frustrating than comforting this time.

"So... you're coming?"

"What?"

"You don't know? I thought I... actually, hold that thought," she said with a grin. "I might not have you for long. Anyway..." she paused, sidling over to Jonathan before planting a kiss on his cheek.

"I couldn't be sure," she giggled, glancing up at Jonathan quickly. "What I was trying to tell you yesterday, before you ran away, and despite all the calls I left..." She was rambling. Still, I had been completely out of it yesterday, and knew ignoring Clara wouldn't help anything.

She paused here.

"Nate kinda asked me out. So..." Clara smiled softly, almost like she needed my approval, but all I felt was shock.

"Umm..."

I knew Clara had feelings for Jonathan, and they had known each other for a while, but I didn't expect anything to actually happen. Jonathan had somehow wormed his way into every part of my life. He was behaving awfully but I couldn't tell Clara that. I felt like I was going insane.

"Emily?"

"That's amazing," I squeaked.

"Well," Jonathan said, "we should probably get going. C?"

"Actually," I exclaimed, "Clara said she'd help me with some Geometry homework?"

His eyes narrowed. "Don't you have detention?"

"Nate," Clara interrupted, "it's fine. Mr. Hale said we could study there instead."

With a smile, and a glower from Jonathan, we were off. I knew I wasn't done with him, not by a long shot, but this was better than nothing. A step in the right direction.

And even though I could hardly bear the thought, I knew Clara wanted me to be happy for her newfound relationship.

"Congratulations with everything," I said, hugging her.

"Thanks," she said with a smile.

I nodded but it wasn't easy to meet her eyes.

"Hey Emily?"

"Yeah?"

"Are you okay?"

"Of course," I said. "I'm fine." As bad as my mood was, being with Clara made it better. She had that effect on people.

"Okay, good," she said, giggling. "We have so much to talk about."

Jonathan might've won this time, but I wouldn't let it happen again.

"We do?" I said, hooking my arm through hers with a smile. "Do tell."

13

BEFORE

It was Monday. A regular day. The beginning of the week, the day most teens dreaded. But for me, I thought I had a purpose. To help Jonathan, despite what was happening, he needed me. What I didn't know was how much I didn't understand. But again, I'm getting caught up in the present.

Back to Monday. Right, a regular day.

"So... how was your weekend?" I asked, tapping Jonathan on the shoulder.

"Fine," he said, flinching. Something was up.

"Seriously? That's it?" I said with a laugh.

He cracked a small smile. "My weekend was fine."

Or maybe it was just me.

"Mine wasn't. Something very strange happened."

"Oh really?" Jonathan asked.

"So after you left I heard someone talking outside my window."

"Oh no, a travesty."

"Jonathan!"

"Okay, okay, don't go all Emily on me. You sure it wasn't a dream?" he replied, grinning slightly. "Or like... a late-night crackhead?"

"I don't know," I replied. "But don't you think that's weird?"

He nodded, but something told me he knew more than he was saying.

"Not be to a downer, but... about Friday?"

The smile melted off Jonathan's face.

"About that, I'm not sure this is a good—" he began.

"Sinclair!"

"Peter? What's he want from you?"

A sigh. "I gotta go, I'll explain later. See you after school?"

"Sure..." I whispered, pushing down the anger that came with Peter. He was *not* friend material. An irritated look from the "man himself" and my feelings solidified. What was Jonathan doing?

~

MY CONFUSION only intensified later that day. Peter was being his usual jerk self, but the strange thing was Jonathan's resignation.

"Kyle, this can't keep happening," Peter's voice hissed from somewhere near me.

I heard a shuffle, a crash, and I was inside an empty classroom, met with a scene that should've been less predictable. Like I've said, Peter is *not* a good person. And what do bad people do? Bully. It's almost unbelievable the amount of times I've walked in on Peter and one of his victims. It made my blood boil every time.

"I—I don't have it, I—"

"I don't care," Peter snapped, pushing the gangly boy, Kyle, back farther into the wall. "You know what happens when—"

"For shit's sake," I exclaimed, pushing my way between them. "What is wrong with you?"

"This has nothing to do with you," he growled back, jerking his head at Jonathan. He wouldn't meet my eyes as he blocked the exit, trapping the four of us inside.

"Jonathan?!"

"I'd suggest leaving." *Peter again.*

"I'm not going anywhere," I snapped, "until you agree to stop being a dick."

I didn't realize Peter had moved until I was pinned against the wall. Pressure spread across my ribs, legs, and face as I slid to the ground. Everything was spinning, darkening, a pain sprouting across my temple. Someone shouted, more shuffling, and a golden blob came into focus. Jonathan glanced down at me, hesitation written across his features. Another shout, and he disappeared.

When the room stopped spinning, I stumbled to my feet, head throbbing. I reached up, and my fingers came away red.

I stumbled outside, into the crowds of students, flowing and confusing my already blurred world.

"Ms. Turner?"

"Uh, yeah?"

"Your temple. What happened, dear? We need to get you to the nurse."

I nodded.

"Who did this to you?"

"Peter," I murmured, regretting the words as they slipped out. He deserved it, but something felt off.

"Peter Lockman?"

"Lockman?"

"Yes, Miss Turner, are you feeling alright? How many fingers am I hold—"

There it was.

"I have to go."

"I'm afraid I can't—"

But I was already gone.

Everything clicked into place, and even in my muddled state of mind, even with my head throbbing and bleeding, I understood. But I was still missing one part of the story: Jonathan's. I needed to find him right away. I couldn't lose Jonathan the way I'd lost everyone else.

I needed him.

14

AFTER

By the time I got home, the relief I'd felt with Clara faded, leaving only dread. I'd tried to stand up to Jonathan, and look how well that'd gone. I'd sent him a text the moment I was alone, and he hadn't responded. I assumed it was part of his torture.

I simply had no way of knowing when he would call, which to me, was another brick added to the pile on my shoulders.

Again, how long had Clara known Jonathan? Did she realize how manipulative he could be? How he tortured his target by not telling me anything? Making me worry constantly? It was too much, and I knew sooner or later I'd have to do something.

My phone buzzed. It was Clara.

Are you ok?

Yeah, why?

Well, you seemed a bit out of it today, is anything up?

This wasn't good.

Clara had a way of telling when something wasn't right, with most things, at least.

I'm fine. Really.

Ok.

But we didn't get a real chance to talk today, I mean, what do you think?

Of you and Jonathan?

Yeah.

He's nice, I typed, pausing as another notification popped up in the corner. This time it was Jonathan.

Did you deliver?

Yes.

I don't see a problem.

He said he wanted to see you. Not me.

Who?

I don't know his name.
Short, dark hoodie, GUN.
I can't do this anymore.

And what exactly do you think will happen if you don't?
What will people think when they find out?
No one will forget.

Why are you doing this?

Because.
I want to.

He wasn't going to stop.

And that final realization weighed me down more anything else had. It pushed me to the ground, stripped away the last fragment of hope I had left.

I set the flip-top against my bed, screen down, buzzes illuminating the covers slightly.

Was all this my fault? Was it pure chance Jonathan was here? That Clara could be this oblivious? That one day years ago had all led to this? Had it all been because of me?

The ringing of an call broke my spiraling chain of thoughts. Almost on instinct, I accepted, silence the only thing answering me.

"What do you want?" I whispered, anger making my words sharp and clipped.

"What do you mean?" Clara's voice snapped back.

"Sorry, I thought—"

"You obviously have something to say!" she interrupted. "You just stopped texting, and you've seemed really weird about Jonathan and me!"

This was it. *Please understand.*

"Clara. Jonathan is *not* who you think he is."

"And how exactly would you know? Met him for—let me think—one week?"

"I'm sorry about this, but I just know. Jonathan is not a good person."

I wanted to say more, but didn't want to involve Clara anymore than she already was. My problems were messed up enough without her.

"*Nate* is kind and generous, and I think you're just jealous."

"Jealous!?" I shouted, voice cracking as I tried to calm myself. "Jonathan is manipulating you!"

"No, he's not! You don't know anything about him, and you never will!"

I exhaled sharply. "That's it, do you know where we *met*, Clara? Jonathan's been to Juvie."

"You don't know anything," she whispered, voice low and distant. "And apparently, I don't know you either."

"Clara!" I shouted, *needing* to show her how wrong she was, but didn't get the chance.

"Bye, Emily."

"*Dammit,*" I muttered, the flip-top falling to the ground with a clatter. I began to laugh, tears of either anger or shame burning my eyes as the emptiness roared inside me. The dark force was wide awake now, claws sharpened and teeth gleaming. Ready to prey on the fears scrambling my insides.

~

Everything was tense. Pulled into knots and pushed away into boxes. The flip-top now lay beside me, silver fractures painted across the screen. I sat in the corner, an old crate in front of me, open and glaringly obvious. A journal sprawled across my lap, blank page open and pen in my hand.

I had lost my only real friend. It was a gaping hole in my heart.

NOTHING HAD CHANGED in the several hours I paced around my room. Jonathan hadn't spoken to me, over call or text, and I knew he was waiting for me to respond. I caved.

Ok.

What do you want me to do?

You're going to the party this Saturday.

I'm going to give you a thumb drive.

And you're going to plug it into a computer.

That's it?

That's it.

And the guy with the gun?

Good luck.

"Perfect," I whispered. "This is just fucking perfect."

I glared at the journal in front of me, blank and inviting. Pen to paper, off again. To my lap, back in the crate. Under my bed, sprawled across the floor. Time ticking by faster and faster.

Broken by Mom's voice.

"You still in the bathroom?"

"No," I hollered back, shoving the crate under my bed as I scrambled to my feet.

The door creaked open, Mom's tired face sticking into my room.

"I picked up Thai."

"I'm not hungry."

Her face crumpled, head tilting and expression changing. *You've done it this time.*

"You have to eat sometime."

"I ate at school."

"Emily!"

"I'm coming," I retorted, following her into the kitchen. Takeout lay haphazardly on the table, surrounded by piles of papers, Mom's greasy apron flung against one of the chairs. She scooped the papers away, but not quickly enough. They looked too official to be sprawled on our table.

I slipped into the opposite chair, pulling the container closer to me. Rich aromas tickled my nose, but all I felt was empty.

"How was your day?" Mom whispered, not-so-subtly slipping the papers into a cabinet.

"Normal."

"Alright," she replied, and even though I wasn't looking at her, I could picture the way her brow knotted, creases crumpling prominently.

"How was school today?"

"You already asked that."

"Oh, that's strange," Mom whispered, features darkening before glancing back to me, face twisting into a strained smile. "I can't believe I forgot the water! I'll be right back."

"Okay," I murmured, trailing her every move as she walked to the faucet.

"Like I was going to say," she continued, slipping back to her seat. "Budget cuts are being made and—not again!—"

Water splashed onto the table, the loud clank of glass hitting the floor.

"Got it," I said, grabbing a rag and wiping down the table as I shot quick glances up at Mom. The more I looked at her, the more I noticed how terrible she looked. Dark smudges circled her eyes, more prominent than usual, face almost gaunt, narrow, nails bitten to stubs as her hands twisted around each other harshly.

"Mom?"

"Yeah?"

"Are you okay?"

Her face broke into that same strained smile as she let out a big sigh.

"Don't worry about me. You're the one in high school! I'm just a little tired." She laughed quickly, squeezing my hand before returning to her seat.

But despite what she said, something wasn't right.

That makes two of us, I thought, faking a smile.

Maybe Jonathan wasn't the only good liar.

15

AFTER

Four days later, I found myself standing in front of the bathroom mirror, wearing a black dress and silver eye shadow that made me look like an alien. I couldn't stop thinking about the fight with Clara, about her blossoming "relationship" with Jonathan, and how weird my own Mom was acting.

I was beginning to wonder if any of this was happening, because it sure didn't seem real. But real or not, I was still expected to go to this party and do a thing I didn't want to do. Hopefully, the black dress would help me go unnoticed.

I shot one glance back at the girl in the mirror before slipping out the bathroom door. I scribbled a hasty note to Mom, which was of course a total lie.

I promised Clara I would help her with some
schoolwork stuff this weekend, so I'm gonna
probably gonna stay the night at her place. Hope
you don't mind.
Love, Em

With that, I pulled a coat around my shoulders and stepped into the night.

~

THE LONGER I WALKED, the colder and colder it got, and I wished I had a car. Fat chance. I didn't even have a license yet. I hadn't even been to *driver's ed*. Again, probably the only sixteen year old ever.

Eventually I reached the address Jonathan had given me, which turned out to be a house where lights pulsed in the windows to the beat of steadily pounding bass.

I glanced around the dark neighborhood before rapping on the door. Muffled voices seemed to reply and then the door swung open, revealing a red-haired boy who might have been 18. He was small for his size though, but when he turned to me like I was a fifth grader, I straightened up.

"Aren't you a little young to be here?"

"Uh—I'm here with Jonath—I mean Nate?"

This changed his demeanor completely, as if I had said the magic word.

"All right," he said, stepping aside to let me pass, revealing a dark room stuffed with sweaty teenagers.

"Thanks," I said, walking slowly into a throng of garbled conversations and ear-splitting music. The pulsing lights seemed to drill into my eyes. The bass made my heart want to skip beats. I felt like a fish lost in a murky sea of tangled legs and waving arms.

"You ready?"

I flinched, whipping around to meet Jonathan's golden hair and cruel smirk.

"Jonathan?"

"Tonight I'm Nate," he whispered, leaning in close as he dropped something cold into my hand. I quickly clenched it tight, stepping away from Jonathan's insincere smile. "You might need this as well."

"Where's the computer?" I muttered back as Jonathan leaned closer and dropped something else into my pocket. A box, maybe?

"Downstairs, first door on your right," he said, words almost lost in the music as he slipped back into the crowd. I followed close behind, heart skipping a beat when he tapped the shoulder of a petite blonde.

Clara turned, her eyes lighting up as she wrapped her arms around him. When she saw me though, her face went dark and she turned away. I stepped forward, then stopped, backing up farther, angry and ashamed.

"Emily!" someone yelled, almost making me cry out in surprise.

It was Mason.

"You almost gave me a heart attack," I snapped, feeling my face turn red. To my surprise, he also seemed embarrassed.

"Sorry, I didn't mean to sneak up on you," he laughed, eyebrows raising as he looked me over.

"It's fine," I mumbled, trying to laugh. Why was I so flustered around this guy? "What were you saying?"

"Oh, I guess it doesn't matter anymore."

"Sorry, I-uh... kinda interrupted you."

He smiled, eyes flickering around the room before meeting mine again. Then the smile disappeared and he beckoned me away from the crowd and into a quiet corner.

"What's wrong?" I said, trying to keep my voice light.

He glanced past me, and I followed his gaze to Clara and Jonathan, confused.

"It's just..." he began, pausing, and biting his cheek softly. "Something's been... I don't know, up, I guess?"

I stepped closer.

"What do you mean?"

"I mean, Nate's been acting weird lately, or... ever since you came here, everything's been strange." He glanced at me, possibly waiting for me to reassure him. But I didn't respond.

"It's like you and Nate are connected, and—and I sound crazy, don't I?"

"You're not crazy."

He nodded halfheartedly as he stared around the room. "It's like Clara's a different person, and Nate is too. Especially around her," he whispered, concern or maybe even anger creeping into his tone, "I just don't like it, y'know?"

"Yeah..." I whispered, surprised. Mason was more perceptive than I thought.

"Sorry," he said, turning back to me, the faraway gaze gone from his eyes, "I totally ruined your night with all these theories. And—"

"No no no," I babbled, nervous energy fidgeting through me. "It's fine."

"I did. This has nothing to do with you, Emily. Um, sorry, hope you have a good night," he said quickly, unnecessarily rushed as he began to back up into the crowd again.

I watched him go, mouth opening and closing with unspoken words as we shared uncertain glances.

"Wait," I muttered softly, knowing Mason was *so* close to the truth. And yet, I got the feeling he wouldn't ask me about it again.

I exhaled, knowing this was my last chance to dispose of the drive. Trying to clear my head, I looked up to find the door Jonathan had mentioned. It was on the far side of the room, hidden behind the swaying heads and limbs of partygoers.

There, I thought, grateful for my height as I ducked and pushed my way to the door. My closed fist and pinched face felt like a beacon, obvious signs I didn't belong.

Glancing behind me, I slipped inside, closing the door with a soft click. I waited a couple seconds, praying the pounding outside was just the music.

I crept down the hall, replaying Jonathan's instructions in my head as I neared the first door. Inside appeared to be a kid's bedroom: superhero posters on the walls, unmade bed, and scattered gaming devices strewn across the room. A desk was pushed into the corner, a black computer closed invitingly, almost like it was waiting for me.

I grabbed the box-like object from my purse, and opened it to find a black iPhone that was small and old, but still way more modern than my flip-top. I crouched down over the computer, the pale light of the monitor contrasting the flashing colors outside as I thought over what I had to do. In a way, it made sense.

The computer needed a password, while surprisingly, the iPhone did not. The Notes app was already open, with several paragraphs written in short sentences. *INSTRUCTIONS,* it read.

The password is Harv1278. Insert the drive, then open and run the application.

My teeth ground together as I typed, resisting the urge to wipe my hands against my dress. There, I was in.

The drive went in smoothly, and after several agonizing seconds I found the application. It looked like a RAT, a remote access tool... at least from what I remembered from the backstreets of STEM summer camp, which felt like a century ago.

Thinking back to those times when I'd actually tried to be happy was always painful, but reminiscing didn't erase reality. Did Jonathan know how experienced I was with tech, or was this just another ploy to get me doubting myself.

Focus.

Anyway, it meant Jonathan wanted to access this computer secretly, something that finally started to put pieces together.

I scanned the computer, occasionally rewriting bits of code according to the written notes, changing settings and running scripts. It was scarily familiar, almost comforting to feel my fingertips gloss over the keys, rewriting the future. I sighed, almost nostalgic as I removed drive, hoping my work would be undetectable by other users.

Finally, I restarted the computer, seconds ticking by as the screen stayed dark, satisfaction as everything returned to its new "normal."

For a moment I thought I was done, *good,* but then I saw even more directions.

Stick the drive into the router.

I scanned the room, eventually finding the flat black rectangle with antennae that had to be the router. Stilling my hands, I racked my memory, trying to remember anything *helpful* about routers, ports, RATs, or anything Jonathan wanted me to do.

Nevertheless, I sat in front of it, carefully waiting until the lights stopped flashing and turned a hopeful green, before stepping back. Now I understood why I needed the iPhone. I checked that everything was running properly, at least as well as I could determine, and carefully typed in the commands. I released a breath when I logged in. *Still got it.*

Someone would suffer for what I'd just done, and while I felt bad for them, I felt even better that my job here was almost done.

One last instruction.

The next couple minutes stretched on like eternity, checking and rechecking every number, letter, or symbol, knowing exactly who I was sending everything to.

"This better be someone you know," I whispered to the screen.

"What are you doing?"

"I—um... I—" I babbled, flipping around to see the red-haired boy I had met at the door.

"I was looking for the bathroom..."

"It's upstairs."

"I—I'm sorry, I've never been here before and..." I stopped, the way his eyes narrowed gave off a strong *don't even think about it* look.

"Consider me gone."

I almost ran out the door and up the stairs, head down as I walked quickly past Clara and Mason. I could feel their gazes boring into my back, ice-cold and piercing.

I rushed out the door, only pausing when the the pulsing of the music disappeared, checking that the drive was still safe in my trembling palm.

16

AFTER

I pocketed the drive, hoping I'd done everything right. Lucky for me, this time I knew what Jonathan was doing, mostly, and now all I had to do was figure out why.

It seemed obvious he planned to use the RAT to contact someone secretly, using me as his access tool. But something was still off, I had to be missing something.

The bright lights of a passing car blinded me, and I flinched as the iPhone clattered to the ground.

"Ugh..." I muttered, that same *off* feeling plaguing me as the iPhone flickered on. The back of my neck prickled, and before I knew what I was doing, I was logged in. My suspicions were confirmed moments later.

An unknown number was texting the computer, a number I instantly recognized as Jonathan's. I stopped, shivers crawling across my arms and legs.

`Is next week a go?`

The computer typed; I assumed it was the person with the gun. Who else was wrapped up in Jonathan's plans?

Yes, she'll have no idea what's happening.

Are you sure she trusts you?

She's wrapped around my finger.
We'll be fine.

And her friend?

Dread curled in my stomach as I realized who they were talking about.

Emily?
She doesn't even know you exist.

Good.
We'll talk more tomorrow.

The typing stopped, and I knew they were gone. I stared at the screen, a pit growing in my stomach as I realized I wasn't the only one Jonathan had roped into this crazy mess. There was no doubt Clara was as well. And yet she still didn't know anything.

This is just getting better and better, I thought. Sucking in a strained breath, I began to walk home. I knew a teenage girl with my mindset shouldn't be out alone at this time of night.

I shivered, speeding up to a jog as the silence closed in.

WHEN I MADE IT HOME, Mom was nowhere to be found. I texted Clara, but she didn't respond. *Understandably. I hadn't exactly been the best friend lately.*

Clara, we need to talk.
I know you don't want to, but there's something you need to know.

THE REST of the night passed without response, and the longer time passed, the more the anxious thoughts grew.

Clara, please respond.
Something terrible is going on and I really need to talk to you.

The next day flew by, with no response from my friend.

Clara. PLEASE.

Finally a response.

Leave me alone.

We need to talk.

Leave me alone.

It's about Jonathan.

LEAVE.

ME.

ALONE.

Since that was all she was going to say, I actually decided to call her. She couldn't ignore me forever, right?

"Emily—for the love of god—leave me alone!"

"Clara, I need to tell—"

"I don't want to hear it! I'm done with you and your stupid theories!" Clara yelled.

"I—" I began, but didn't get the chance to finish.

" I. DON'T. CARE."

She hung up, and according to the phone, we'd only talked for 12 seconds.

Anger burned through me, the flip-top sweaty, clenched tight in my hand. I felt the urge to throw it, watch it shatter with satisfaction against the wall, but I restrained myself. It was the only way I could contact Clara, or Jonathan it seemed, at least for now.

SUNDAY NIGHT, Monday at school or after, nothing from Clara. I'd tried to find her between classes, but it was nearly impossible. Whenever I saw her, Jonathan would be there, or she'd be surrounded by a group. And for what I needed to tell her, we had to be alone.

Now it was Tuesday, and even though my anxiety was near breaking point, I couldn't let Mom find out what I was feeling.

"Have a good day," she said, dropping me in front of the school.

"I'll try," I whispered, sending back the same strained smile as I got out of the car. Waving weakly, I approached the building, trying to ignore my nerves as I scanned my surroundings for Clara.

Instead, Jonathan approached, tell-tale smirk smeared across his face.

"Did you dispose of the phone?"

"What?"

"The last item on the list. On Notes?"

I couldn't believe what had happened. Jonathan didn't know I still had the phone. Or that I could see his texts.

"Yeah. I left it by the computer."

His eyes narrowed, I raised my eyebrows, and hoped he couldn't tell that the iPhone wasn't by the computer. In fact, it was stuffed in the backpack slung across my shoulder right then.

"Do you know where Clara is?" I asked.

"At her locker...? Why?" he muttered.

"Thanks."

He snorted, rolling his eyes as I took a breath, bypassing my locker before finding Clara's. Mustering my courage, I tapped her on the shoulder.

"Do you not know what 'leave me alone' means?"

"Please let me talk," I said, speaking to her turned back.

"Emily—"

"Please."

She turned around, mouth a tight line, but didn't walk away.

"There's something I haven't told you," I began, knowing this was my only chance to talk. I needed to focus.

"And?"

"Well... can we talk privately?"

She rolled her eyes and dragged me to the girls' bathroom, checking under the stalls before turning back to me.

I froze at Clara's irritated look, my head telling me to leave, but my gut saying the opposite. Her brows rose impatiently.

"Well? Talk."

"Before I moved here, I was a different person, and—I..." *Come on, Emily.*

"Spit it out."

"I'm not a nice person, Clara." I didn't know how to *begin* to tell her about what Jonathan had done. How he'd held my life over my head for weeks, how he'd tore Clara and I apart, how he'd even threatened to reveal the subject I never wanted to talk about. Ever.

"I'm a criminal," I blurted, dropping the journal on the floor in front of us.

"Yeah, right," Clara laughed insincerely. "You? Hilarious."

"I'm serious. Peter Lockman, November 21st, the reason I went to therapy... and Juvie."

"What?"

"I... we got into a fight," I muttered, almost quiet enough to be intelligible, but by the way Clara's face changed from disbelief to fear, I knew she'd hear me.

"Who are you?" Clara whispered, eyes wide and voice low.

I laughed, strained and loud, too loud, as I flipped open the journal.

Clara flinched.

"Do you want the short version or the long one?"

17

BEFORE

I had searched for almost ten minutes, and Jonathan was nowhere to be found. What didn't help was the never-ending stream of students, my increasing panic, and the constant throbbing in my head.

Ten more minutes passed, then twenty, forty, and the final bell. I was dejected, panicked, and on the verge of tears. I needed air. Seconds later, I was through the nearest door, stumbling out into whipping winds.

I could breathe again.

When the world stopped spinning, I opened my eyes again, and now I wasn't just panicked. I was pissed. And of course that's when Jonathan appeared, as if in a dream.

"Jonathan," I shouted, stopping so we were face to face. Close. "We need to talk."

"Emily..." he whispered, voice wobbling and face tear-streaked. "Right now really isn't a good time."

"Oh really, 'cause this," I pointed at my temple, "was not something I planned for today."

"I'm sorry but—"

"Yeah, I bet you're sorry."

"*Em.*"

"Exactly how many times did you lie to me?"

He flinched at this.

"You really didn't think I'd found out about Lockman?"

"Please, Em."

"All you've done is lie to me the entire time we've known each other, and now this? Watching as your 'employer' beats me up for helping his victim? You really expect me to forget this? I can't even—"

"Stop, *please.*"

"No, Jonathan. What is wrong with you? Why would—"

"STOP!" he shrieked, grabbing my wrists with crazed eyes. "Please, **stop**, Emily."

"I—"

"My sister died."

"Oh."

"It doesn't matter," Jonathan spat, dropping my wrists as he backed away. "Because... because I'm just a liar, right?"

"Jonathan—"

"Plus, it definitely doesn't matter that Peter was helping me, right? That maybe I *needed* him for her," he whispered, scarily quiet as he sunk to the ground. "You can't imagine how hard it's been for us. My health didn't matter. My *life* doesn't matter. Lena mattered... I can't, I won't, I..."

"I didn't know," I said, slipping next to him silently.

"I can't do this anymore," he sobbed, crunching his legs closer to his chest. "I can't I can't I can't."

"I'm so sorry."

"No," Jonathan whispered, stumbling to his feet. "No, you're not. You wouldn't have said that if you were."

"Wait, that's not what—"

"No, Emily," he said, pulling back even farther. "Get away from me."

"Jonathan—"

"No." His voice was tortured, face blank and puffy. "Go away!" Jonathan backed up, a darkness in his eyes as he turned his back. "Leave, and don't *ever* come back."

"I..."

But Jonathan was gone. Wiped from existence just as fast as I'd found him.

My eyes stung, a gaping loneliness threatening to swallow me. My first friend, first something, was gone. I had pushed everyone so far they just... broke.

This was how it always went.

These kinds of things are always my fault. Right? I never mattered enough for someone to stay. And even if they were parentally obliged to? No. I can see them once, twice maybe.

I do not deserve their friendship.

And yet, none of this would have happened if not for Peter. It was always easier to blame someone else for your problems, but this time maybe it really *was* Peter. And I knew where to find him.

Grim satisfaction flew through me as I saw him, right outside in the alley, just as I remembered.

"PETER!"

He turned, eyebrow raised as I stalked towards him. He wasn't expecting me this time.

A crash and we were on the ground. Punches flew, hot, angry, kicks, flailing, then... a crack. The world returned to its normal color, at least until I looked around and saw red. Everywhere.

I shrieked, pushing myself as far from that red as I could before the footsteps and the hushed breath. I turned, fear splashing through me as I saw him.

I WOULD NEVER FORGET what happened that night. It changed me. A horrible, traumatic change, but… I can't even come up with an excuse. Damaged could've been the right word.

It was by far, the worst thing that has ever happened to me. At least, it used to be.

PART 3

18

AFTER

Clara stared at me, expression shifting as she grabbed my hand. "We can't talk here," she said.

"Where then?"

She didn't answer, but the tight grip of her hand said plenty. We slipped out the door as Clara dragged me down the hall and into an empty classroom.

She tugged me to a corner, pulling down until we sat face to face.

"Okay," she whispered, all hints of cold persona gone, "*what* are you talking about?"

"I guess we should start back before I moved."

"Moved?"

"Yeah, from L.A," I said, realizing Clara really didn't know that much about me. Her forehead crinkled, apparently noticing the same thing.

"I've lived in L.A. for most of my life, and I mean, I wasn't the "perfect" kid back then. I was... violent."

Our eyes met, and I glanced back down at my sneakers.

"So I went to a new school, and there was this one guy, Peter," I continued, flashing back to that fateful night. "He was a bully. He always picked on the younger kids, and one day I'd had enough of it. We got into a fight and... Jonathan was there but he left shortly, and I guess *I* called 911. I don't remember. I watched him for a while, but left as soon as I heard the sirens. Fear paralyzed me, Clara. I didn't know what to do..." I glanced back up at her, dreading the look on her face. Too blank.

"Then what?"

Her voice was emotionless, an eery echo of her face.

"I assume 911 arrived. When I got home, Mom asked me a bunch of questions, and I guess I was in shock. I couldn't seem to speak. Peter was comatose for three months. During that time I was sentenced to spend the year afterwards in the nearest Juvenile Detention Center. I was released a year later, and we moved here." I laughed. "Needed a new start, I guess."

"Is that it?" Clara whispered, a slight tremble cracking through her voice.

"No."

"Something about Na—uh, Jonathan?"

I nodded. Clara didn't say anything, but I could see the doubt and despair battling in her eyes.

"I have this... habit where I write everything down. Happened after therapy, so when I tell you about him, you need to believe me." I whispered, displaying my journal with shaking hands. I wasn't sure if she'd believe me without solid proof, and this was as close as I'd get.

Her eyes widened as she flipped through the pages of my journal, reading my darkest thoughts and actions. There was a reason I'd kept them so hidden. My ears burned; I didn't want Clara to see what I'd written about her, Mason, or Jonathan.

She stopped after the first couple pages. "Is this true?"

Guilt coiled in my gut, but I continued.

"The first day we met, during lunch, I recognized Jonathan. At first, he didn't seem to recognize me, but then... he did. That's when everything changed for the both of us. Jonathan knew, and he threatened to tell everyone about Peter if I didn't do what he wanted. So I did."

"Seriously?" Clara croaked, voice wobbling slightly.

"I'm sorry, Clara. But Jonathan *definitely* isn't who you think he is. He's been blackmailing me for weeks, and..." I looked back up at her, almost leaving my sentence at that. "He's been manipulating you, too." A pause. "You can read more if you want."

Clara squeezed her eyes shut tight, crumpling her features as she blinked back tears. I sat there quietly, unsure how to comfort her when it was partially my fault. Her life had been perfect before me.

She inhaled deeply, wiping the back of her hand across her face, before her eyes flashed to mine. For a second, I thought I could see a flicker of something so tortured it chilled me to the bone, but seconds later, it was gone. Only pools of ice blue stared back at me.

"You're insane," Clara declared, knocking my journal across the floor. She stumbled to her feet, eyes flickering around the empty chairs and dimmed lights. "Everyone in this goddamned school is insane."

Her words hit me like a truck, my chest clenching as breath escaped my lungs with a choked gasp.

She glanced back at me, eyes filled with fear and betrayal as she rushed past. The door slammed shut, leaving my shaking body curled on the ground, gasping like a fish out of water. Tears blurred my eyes as the world tipped and spun.

Maybe this is it.

Swirling and twirling, colors began to fade from the room, focusing and unfocusing on the images in front of me.

Maybe I should've stayed locked away.

Partial faces, wide smiles, cruel smiles, slight ones, crooked ones, ones stopped mid-laugh. Dark rooms, bright rooms, rooms so small you could touch both walls with outspread hands.

She should've left too.

Younger memories wrapped around me, deliciously light and warm as I looked up into Mom's face. She smiled and hugged me close, that feeling threatening to yank me far from the living world. To drift away into the warmth and light, and never wake up again.

"Emily!" a voice shouted, almost breaking through the warmth. "Emily, please. Breathe."

I opened my eyes, Mom's face shifting into a dark-haired one.

Breathe, I wasn't breathing.

"Mason?" I croaked, air whooshing through my lips.

His face cracked into a faint smile, pulling me closer. The world spun back into focused color, and I realized the warmth surrounding me were his arms.

"What happened?"

"Please leave," I whispered, pushing him away as I tried to stand. "I have to—whoa." Spinning, spinning, spinning.

"Emily. What happened?"

"Mason, please."

"I can't just leave."

My chest tightened again, and I grabbed onto Mason for balance. His face broke, worry and fear splashing across it like paint on a canvas. Tears began to pour down my cheeks as my face flushed hot with emotion. The world began to blur as I rallied my strength, pushing through Mason's arms and darting down the hall, journal in hand. I didn't know when I'd picked it up.

I ran down the halls, faster and faster, trying to ignore the tightening in my chest. It became unbearable, a burning that spread from my lungs to my legs. I didn't even register the pain as I crashed into my locker.

My scant tears had evolved into sobs now, muddying the brain and confusing my body. It was getting harder and harder to breathe, and I felt like choking right then, going back to that warmth and forgetting about everything. I only had—

"Ms. Turner? Are you alright?"

I stopped. "I'm fine."

"Alright..." Mr. Hale murmured, and I could tell he didn't believe me one bit. "Before you leave, your essay on self-reflection was due yesterday."

"Oh, right," I mumbled, struggling to repress tears as I shuffled through my locker. I flung my journal to the very back. I'd *never* let anyone see it again. "Here."

"Wonderful. And you're sure you're alright?"

"Yep."

"Okay. I hope you've learned your lesson," he said, shaking the paper slightly. "I hope I don't ever see you in detention again."

I nodded, a strange feeling settling over me as I left. Mr. Hale didn't know how right he was. I had a feeling I'd never see him—in or out of detention— ever again. Strangely, it was a comforting thought.

By the time I reached my house, the rain had stopped and the sky was a dark, depressing color, almost as if it were reflecting my mood. I hadn't seen Mom's car in the parking lot, which seemed better, as I was *not* in the mood to talk to anyone.

The door swung shut with a sharp click behind me as my heart skipped a beat. Mom was at the table, a tall, dark-haired woman sitting across from her. But what made me stop was the papers strewn about the table, big, red letters stamping out the words:

Eviction Notice

19

AFTER

"What?" I exclaimed. Mom's face seemed to age decades in moments. The woman next to her looked like she would rather be anyone else.

"I'll be–"

"Mom," I whispered, tight and controlled as I slipped next to her. "Who is this?"

"This is Ms. Lenards. She's our landlord, and I guess I should've told you earlier but..."

"What?"

"Honey, I haven't paid rent for a while and Ms. Lenards was just here to remind me about it."

Ms. Lenards shot Mom a glance, before looking back to me awkwardly. "I think I'd better leave. But about these papers..."

"I know," Mom whispered, standing shakily. "By the end of the month."

Ms. Lenards nodded, grabbing a small briefcase before disappearing out the door.

"Mom," I said, scooting into the chair next to her. "How long has it been since we paid?"

"You don't need to worry about this. I'll find a—"

"Mom."

"Six months," she whispered.

"Oh."

"I didn't want to tell you, but—"

"No, I get it," I said blankly. "But, what happens at the end of the month?"

A sigh. "We'll get kicked out."

"Like homeless, out?"

"Emily," she whispered, reaching across to clasp my hands. "We'll figure something out."

"I'm sorry," I gasped, my chest beginning to tighten.

"Emily–"

"I can't."

Stumbling, tears flowing down my face for the second time that day, I ran to my room. I threw the window open, cold air whisking into the empty space that felt less like a place I would live in than ever before. It was coldest near the ground so I slumped there, enjoying the chill.

"Hey Em," a voice whispered.

HE BROUGHT his fingers to his lips in the universal "shhh" sign, before shuffling next to me. I could feel his hot breath on my ears, unwanted in a way that kept me frozen stock-still.

"If you scream—if you make any sound—I swear I'll report your mother."

"What?"

He smirked, dread pooling in my stomach as he leaned closer.

"You really shouldn't have come back. With your house, that

money situation, and the drugs," Jonathan drawled. "This really isn't looking too good for you."

"What are you talking about?"

"Oh Em," he whispered back, reaching behind him with a grin.

A faint glow lit up the room as Jonathan turned on his phone, fingers trembling and eyes glimmering almost as if he had made it himself. He flipped past several photos, each one showcasing white powdered bags, suspiciously large syringes and pictures of our house in the background. Specifically, Mom's nightstand.

"CPS wouldn't like this."

No. He couldn't do that. I would lose... everything. My future, the house, Mom. NO.

"Yeah, but these aren't real."

I didn't realize I had spoken until Jonathan snorted, smugness practically oozing from every word.

"Child Protective Services won't know that," he said. "'I was visiting my friend's house, and I knew she was struggling with anxiety and *destructive* tendencies, when I found this. My family had a history with drug use, and... I *had* to help her, I mean, wouldn't anyone?'"

As he spoke, I kept my eyes on the screen, irritated by the smirk on his face.

"Why would you... how..."

His face curled into a smile, and that's when I realized Jonathan would had *never* given up his "substance" dealing. He'd clearly found new clients and a partner to boot.

I gritted my teeth, hard. Even after Lena had passed, he wouldn't stop. And now he had the nerve to blackmail *me?* With the very same trade that took him away from Lena in her final moments?

No. I wouldn't let him ruin the last person I had left.

Anger thrummed through my veins, turning my vision that

telltale red as I lunged forward. We crashed to the ground, Jonathan's grunt of surprise fueling me further. I tried to pin him down, but he was larger, and stronger, but with a calculated shove his phone skidded across the floor.

I shot forward, fingers barely grasping the phone before I was yanked back, pain flashing through my temple.

Jonathan leapt to his feet, looking down at me with hardened eyes and flushed cheeks. "Get up," he growled.

I scrambled to my feet, fear flashing through me as I tried to guess what Jonathan was thinking. *Did I push him too far?*

He glared, grabbed me firmly by the hand, pulling me so close I almost gagged at his sickly-sweet stench. It was not *normal.*

"We're going to walk through the house to the door," he whispered, hand tightening harder against my arm. "You're going to tell your mom that I came over to help with a school project, and we're going to go pick something up from my house."

"My Mom will never believe that."

He waved the phone slightly as I felt the excuse shrivel and die on my lips. "Okay."

"Don't make a sound," he said, pausing to squeeze my arm even harder than before. "Understand?"

I nodded, pushing back tears as Jonathan dragged me through the door and into the hallway. He glanced at me, the pressure on my arm increasing as we approached the kitchen.

"Mom?" I called tentatively, trying to keep the tremble out of my voice. "My friend came over and—" I stopped, paralyzed.

Her limp form was slumped across the floor, head lolling and skin dangerously pale and glazed with sweat. I yanked away from Jonathan, collapsing next to her as tears began pouring down my face again.

"Mom," I whispered, shaking her shoulders gently at first, then harder and harder as she stayed limp. "Mom, can you hear me? Are you okay?"

She didn't move. I grabbed her hands, clammy and far too cold. Something was seriously wrong.

I whipped around,"Did you *do* something?"

"We have to leave," Jonathan growled, grabbing my arm again.

"Let go of me!"

"We're leaving."

"Get *out* of my house!" I yelled, thrashing and kicking until I heard a muffled grunt. I jumped to my feet, dashing across the room and slamming my bedroom door shut behind me, shoving a chair underneath the handle.

"911. What's your emergency?"

"It's my Mom! She's unconscious and not responding to anything. We live on Snider Avenue at Penning Street. Please hurry, I don't—"

In the next instant, I was knocked down, breath crushed out of my lungs with a thud. The flip-top crashed next to me, shattering into pieces. Gone. Jonathan kicked it away, yanking me off the ground as he dragged me toward the door.

"Jonathan, I can't just leave her without—"

"Shut up," he whispered hoarsely, and if I looked closely, I could see his face pale. I shoved back my sobs, eyes not leaving Mom's broken body until the door slammed behind us.

Jonathan's grip was tight as we exited, and despite my struggles, he held strong. I knew it was pointless when we disappeared into the darkness with only cold stars to light our path. The dark force plunged its claws into my mind, anger fading into fear as it pushed me forward with a shaking body and frozen brain.

I couldn't stop him.

20

AFTER

Jonathan led me through dark alleyways and side streets at a fast pace, only stopping to glance back every once in a while. It should've seemed strange, except I was so caught up in my thoughts, trying to find a way out of this mess, that I didn't notice.

"Where are we going?" I whispered shakily, trying to stay as far from Jonathan as humanly as possible.

He didn't respond. Instead, he clenched my arm tighter as we rushed down a dim alley filled with overturned boxes and dumpsters. It seemed familiar. We turned down another alley, slowing to a halt in front of a deteriorated house, layered in shadows and grime.

It took me several more moments before I realized where we were going. When I did, any willpower to continue shriveled up and died. My knees locked, sweat beaded at my brow as another wave of intense trembling set over me.

"Emmmm," Jonathan whispered, trying to cover laced words with an airy tone. "Let's go."

"Are you sure we... *okay*."

He opened the door, pushing me into the dust-covered halls of the house where'd I'd first met Jonathan's accomplice. My eyes locked onto every dark corner or covered space as Jonathan led me past the kitchen and into a dark room.

It had the same barred windows, and the floors were still layered in dust, but there was nothing else in the room except for a rusty metal chair. I turned to Jonathan, his face layered with shadows, teeth glinting as I realized what he was going to do.

He twisted his body, stepping one foot behind me, and before I knew what was happening, I was jerked upwards, slamming back down into the chair. Moments later, I was trapped. Tied to the chair with vise-like precision, Jonathan left me to my metallic prison.

"What are you doing?!" I shrieked, struggling against the rope pointlessly. It was far too tight to wriggle out of.

"Hey hey hey... you don't want to wake anybody up, do you?"

"Jonathan," I hissed, glaring at what I thought was his dark form. It was so dark and dusty I could hardly see him standing right in front of me.

"Anything you want to say to Clara?"

"Clara?!"

He didn't respond. Instead, the room lit up with a bright rectangle of light, a quiet ring freezing the words on my lips.

"Hello?" said Clara's disembodied voice.

"Hey babe," Jonathan said. "I'll be there in a couple minutes."

"Oh, okay."

"Something wrong?" Jonathan asked.

"It's just... something happened with Emily today and—"

I tried not to scream as she spoke my name, but a soft whisper escaped anyway. Jonathan whipped around, fixing me with a glare before approaching the only exit.

"I'm not sure what to do... we'll talk soon?"

"Yeah."

Where are you doing? I mouthed, hoping he could see me through the dark. Jonathan waved, stepped backwards, and with a click, the door was shut, plunging me into complete darkness.

"Damnit!" I spat, glaring at the door as if it would collapse on its own.

The bonds cut deep into my skin as I felt the world around me start to tighten. The harder I pulled against my restraints, the tighter they got. Blue spots eventually made their way into the corners of my eyes, replacing what I thought was the faint outline of a person.

Small streaks of shadow interrupted the yellow light under the door, and mixed with the blue spots, it only made the pain worse. Were those boots? Had Jonathan sent someone to hurt me even more?

"Arhh," I exhaled sharply, freezing as I realized the silence was broken.

The figure shifted, boards creaking as a hushed voice spoke.

"Emily?"

"I'm in here!"

It felt good to raise my voice. Why hadn't I thought of that before? Footsteps approached the door, before a large crash as someone tried to force it open.

Please let it be someone I know. Please let me go back to Mom and wake up from this nightmare.

Several more tries, and with a crunch, the door sagged to the side as a tall form staggered into the room.

"Mason?" I whispered cautiously.

"Oh my god, Emily," he answered, before quickly working on the bonds behind me. "I—what..."

"What are you doing here?" I asked. Don't get me wrong, I was glad he was here, but *why* was he here? It seemed a little too perfect, like something that might happen in a movie.

"After I saw you at school, I was really worried, so I found Clara but she wouldn't tell me anything—which is weird for her—so I tried talking to Nate instead." He paused, letting out a sigh. "But he called someone before I could catch up, and it totally wasn't normal and mentioned you? Something wasn't right, so I followed him and..."

"I know the rest."

"Yeah."

He was untying the ropes as he spoke. Finally, they fell to the ground, and seconds later I was up.

"Can you try calling Clara?" I whispered. Despite Mason's confused glance, he dialed anyway.

Ring.

Ring.

Ring.

"Hello?"

Damn it, I thought, when Jonathan's voice answered the phone.

"Mason?" Jonathan said.

"Nate?" Mason said, glancing at me worriedly. "Why'd *you* pick up?"

"Oh, Clara and I are hanging out."

Despite his nonchalant voice, I still shuddered, especially as Mason's face dawned to one of understanding.

What should I do? he mouthed silently.

"Mason?" Jonathan asked.

Ask about Clara, I mouthed.

What?

"Clara," I whispered, my gestures becoming more and more frantic as the seconds ticked by.

"Where are you?" Mason finally asked.

“Just at her house, though I’d prefer if it was just me and her... you feel me?”

“Yeah, let her know I called,” Mason murmured, staring at me with wide eyes.

“Okay, bye.”

“See you,” Mason said, but Jonathan was already gone.

“Clara’s in trouble, isn’t she?” Mason whispered tentatively. I hesitated but he deserved to know.

“Yes. Jonathan has her.”

He inhaled sharply, grimacing as he turned away. “I can’t believe this is happening.”

“I—”

“I mean I *knew* something was wrong after that phone call, but... this?” His voice faltered as the dark force curled tighter around my gut. “You can’t just *kidnap* people!”

“Mason,” I whispered, turning him so we were face to face. “I wish I could help, but...”

“Tell me what the *hell* is happening?!”

“We don’t have time,” I cried. “You’re going to have to trust me.”

He looked up, and I could see his mind racing, deciding what to do.

“Please.”

“I do,” he finally said with a smile. “I’ll always be here for you.”

I smiled, taking Mason’s hand as we left this nightmarish house. We ran into dim night, on the way to Clara, to Jonathan, to end this.

“Thank you, Mase,” I whispered to myself, glancing back at Mason’s confident figure, knowing that we had *actually* had a chance this time.

A chance, I thought, warmth blossoming inside me. Jonathan didn’t know what was coming.

21

AFTER

"Where are we going?"

"Jonathan picked up when you called Clara, so I'd assume her house," I huffed, slowing momentarily to catch my breath.

"But doesn't that seem a little too... predictable?"

"How so?"

"Well," Mason said, taking hold of my sleeve as we stopped. "I mean, if Nate has Clara—" he stopped, recovering, "—wouldn't he bring her somewhere else?"

"Oh, yeah. Where do you think he would... ?" I trailed off, studying Mason's bedraggled form, searching him for anything *off*. He was Jonathan's friend, after all.

"Okay, so this kinda sounds crazy, but... what if she's at school?" He finally said.

"School?"

"It's quiet, I know Nate breaks in sometimes for a thrill. Clara's parents are super strict about boys, and I know she's always wanted to go with him, *and* now that they're dating..." Mason trailed off.

I nodded, the more I thought it over, the more it made a sort of disturbing, twisted sense.

"It's also nighttime. The school will definitely be empty, too." Mason said, pausing. I could tell it even took him a moment to understand the full implications behind his words.

"So we shouldn't go to Clara's?"

He glanced up at me, nodding slightly.

"Okay," I murmured, changing the route in my head as we began running again. *I'm trusting you,* I thought, glancing back at Mason doubtfully. He smiled faintly, all dimples and white teeth.

I shook my head, with what had happened with Clara and Jonathan, they'd made me paranoid.

Still, I thought. *What could you do?*

~

By the time we arrived outside Westview High School, only two cars filled the parking lot, accompanied by the yellow largeness of the school busses. It almost felt like a mechanical graveyard, something I definitely didn't need to be thinking about.

"Where do you think they are?" I whispered, moving closer to Mason.

"Probably in the gym." *Specific.* "Harder to see the lights, right?"

"Right," I murmured, starting as I felt large hands wrap around mine, warm breath billowing above my head.

"We can do this," Mason whispered, squeezing my hands tightly.

"Yeah," I said, unable to shake the dark force curling tighter around my suspicions.

"See that light?"

"Let's go," I said, creeping towards the front door.

We slipped through the doors, barely making any noise as we approached the gym with its muted, gold light.

"I'll go through the back door."

"Wait, there's a back—" I whispered, turning towards Mason, but he'd disappeared. *"Okay."*

I paused, taking a breath before leaning against the door, inching it open. Where was Clara? Was Mom even okay? Was Mason really trustworthy? Too many unanswered questions. I shook my head, thinking was getting me nowhere.

The gym was empty, or at least, it was the first time I scanned it. Any chairs had been pushed to the sides, plastic crates shoved up against the walls as well. Jonathan, Mason, or Clara were nowhere to be seen.

Steeling myself, I slid into the room, closing the door quietly behind me as I tried to stay unseen. I moved slowly, trying to take in all of the room as I continued forward.

"You know I can see you, right?"

I froze, eyes flickering around the room until I landed on a dark corner to the far right. A flash of movement, and Jonathan walked out of the shadows, stopping several yards away.

"Honestly," he said. "I'm surprised you're here."

He didn't look it. Nonchalance practically radiated off him, head tilted slightly to the right as he studied me. Jonathan glanced behind him (towards the door or the corner, I couldn't tell), but his face changed almost imperceptibly. Annoyance rippled through me—we outnumbered him two to one. He couldn't *do* anything.

"Where's Clara?"

Jonathan's brows raised, almost like he were confused. Had we gone to the wrong place? "Clara?"

"I know she's here with you."

"And why would I care?"

I sighed, glaring. "Clara? Your girlfriend? The one you've

kidnapped? Seriously, what stops me from calling the police right now?"

"Well," Jonathan said, bringing out his own phone, "it isn't too hard make a phone call, and then it's just a matter of how CPS interprets things."

The photos.

"No one's going to believe you. Especially 'cause of of our... you know."

"Never say never," he smiled big, sighing theatrically. "But remember, who's the one that overheard your little family... conversation?"

He couldn't bring Mom into this. But with the eviction notice, the photos, my past, it all made too much sense.

Fuck it.

I reached for the flip-top, but dread splashed through me as I realized it was at home, broken.

"I'd suggest staying still," Jonathan said with a laugh, shouting something unintelligible behind him.

The sound of metal against metal screeched loudly, a small, hooded figure dragging a chair into the room. The figure spun the chair around, my heart almost stopping as I saw Clara. She wasn't moving.

"What the hell did you do?!" I screeched, starting forward, but Jonathan's outstretched arm stopped me. He nodded to the side, and I jumped as I saw a gun aimed point-blank at Clara's forehead. Saying I froze would've been an understatement.

"Don't you love her?" I seethed.

He sighed. "Emmmmm, you should've known better."

"Why are you—what do you even—" my voice cracked as tears welled in my eyes yet again.

"I want you *gone.*" Jonathan's face darkened at his words, something far different from the facade or the taunting smirks. He gestured at the hooded figure, and the gun dropped from Clara's forehead.

"Are you sure?" The person growled, and another shock of adrenaline rushed through me. It was the very same hooded figure that had threatened me weeks ago! I should've guessed.

"Do it!" Jonathan shouted, his voice straining as he turned on his heel and strode toward Clara and the hooded figure. The man muttered, his gun moving to my head for the second time that month.

My facade broke—all of the anger, fear, and desperation escaping my carefully constructed psyche. It pushed me forward with a feeling akin to flying, hundreds of emotions everywhere. I was immensely powerful when I stopped caring about what happened to me.

Jonathan couldn't *control* me anymore. I smiled.

"Stop," the figure growled, shining metal of the gun drawing closer and closer, "I'd prefer to keep this gun loaded."

I didn't stop.

"Do I have to do everything myself?!" Jonathan shouted, pulling a dark pair of gloves from his pocket, thrusting them on angrily as he stalked toward the figure.

He grabbed the gun, pushing the cloaked figure back. Surprise flew through me as the man's hood fell off, revealing the red-head from the party. The one who'd walked in on me with the flash drive.

But now the gun was trained on my head.

"You have *everything* to lose," Jonathan hissed, jerking Clara's chair.

"And you don't?"

He grimaced, nodding at the redhead before turning back to me with a bang. Time seemed to speed up and slow down at the same time.

The bang ricocheted throughout the room, pain stabbing into my ears as a dark-haired blur jumped into me. I was knocked to the ground, a weight pushing on my chest.

The room spun, a smear of light separating into two very different faces. Jonathan was the first, eyes wide and jaw open, gun by his side, and the second: a dark-haired, dark-clothed boy.

Mason.

Scarlet was everywhere, me, Mason, splattered across the floor.

"How could you?" I whispered, taking in the almost perfect crimson circle shot straight through Mason's stomach. There was so much blood, far too much for a single human being to produce?

Mason coughed, red and labored, and before I knew what was happening I was on top of him, hoping the pressure of my hands was enough to stop the flow.

"Mason? Please stay still," I cried, all the doubts I had about him leaking away in the crimson streams.

"I didn't want you to get hurt," he wheezed, dark eyes brimming with tears of either pain or sorrow, I couldn't tell.

"Mase, oh god," I sobbed, curling tighter against him. "I'm so sorry."

"You're doing everything you—"

"This changes things." It was Jonathan.

"What the hell is wrong with you?" I yelled as Jonathan neared, skirting around the pools of red before crouching next to Mason.

"I never meant for you to get hurt," he whispered, almost sincere, before jumping to his feet, phone cocked in an instant. He dismissed the wide-eyed red-head with a wave of his hand, almost like they were master and servant, not high schooler and adult. It seemed when Jonathan was around, the redhead's personality changed completely from the man in the old house. With the squeak of sneakers against the floor, he was gone, out the door and into the night. Except this time he couldn't hide, like Jonathan had. I knew him and his house, at least that was something.

"How could you think no one would get hurt," I said, repressing the urge to yell.

Jonathan didn't answer. He was currently shouting into his phone.

"Oh god please she has a gun, Mason—he's on the ground and my girlfriend, there's white powder and she's not breathing, and I—"

"Where are you?"

Jonathan's response was quick, fake sobs far too convincing. He hung up.

He turned to us, all acting wiped from his face, completely blank, eerily lifeless.

"Okay," Jonathan began, the deadness replaced by a smirk as he dropped the gun to the ground, kicking it across the floor, "I believe this brings the night to an end."

Yeah right, I thought, twisting my foot as I kicked the gun through crimson, and with slight adjustments, it was pointing at Jonathan. There was no way he could pin this on me.

"Don't," Mason said.

"What?" I murmured, taking my eyes off Jonathan for *only* a moment, but when they returned, he was several feet away from the exit.

"Stop!"

Jonathan turned, smiling with a look so sincere it chilled me. "I'll always be here," he whispered, tapping his head slightly. "Goodbye Em, and good luck."

He was gone.

With the plink of a door, the gym was plunged into complete silence.

"We don't have a lot of time," Mason said, lips barely moving, face sweaty and pale.

"Don't speak," I said.

"The gun... Clara," he wheezed, "... he was wearing gloves."

The gun dropped to the floor with a clang.

"A perfect plan," I whispered, the twisted puzzle pieces finally clicking together into a sickly image.

Clara, the parcels, the syringe, photos, lifeless looks, 911... framing me for everything.

Mason nodded, sweaty fingers pulling weakly at my hand pressed against his stomach.

"What are you doing?" I said.

He smiled, letting his hand fall back to the ground. "Clara needs your help."

"I can't just leave you."

"I'm not going anywhere," he whispered.

"If I leave—"

"I know."

"Mason—"

"She needs you now," his voice was so weak and tired. "And Emily, just let me..." A cough. "Nate can't get away, and I trust you. You mean so much to me, and—"

"I know," I said. "I know."

"I can't, we won't forget you, Emily. I—I promise," he murmured, looking up at me with a weary smile. "I know you can do it. We all know it." He stopped, a heavy sigh, his eyes fluttering shut.

I was breaking apart.

"I can't, Mase," I breathed, choking on nothing as I leaned over, wrapping him in a hug. "I—I—" Struggling, I pushed back tears. Standing up, I forced my eyes away from him. "I'm so sorry."

I sniffled, racing over to Clara, trying to ignore my scarlet hands and Mason's stained image.

Clara wasn't looking too good, either. Her skin was tinted blue, faint shivers racking her body, skin hot to the touch.

"What did he do to you?" I gasped, lifting her off the chair and onto the floor. Her pulse too slow, and anger shocked through me as I found the red puncture over her vein. I knew Jonathan had access to opioids, or something similar, but to use them on *Clara?*

She stirred, the shivers increasing so I held her tighter. I wouldn't let my first *real* friend go anytime soon. Clara was so innocent and wonderful. She didn't deserve any of this.

I held her for what could've been minutes or hours, eyes shut tight and tears leaking, hoping to god that her pulse, while slow, wouldn't be the same as Mason's.

"Place the girl on the ground and put your hands in the air!" a gruff voice shouted, bright lights sweeping the room, the familiar whine of sirens fading back into focus. I didn't let go.

Hands jostled me, pulling and pushing until Clara's shuddering body was pulled away. My eyes burst open, blurry and puffed, my arms forced behind my back, cold metal locking them in place.

"What's your name, young lady?"

When I didn't answer, the hands jostled me more.

"Emilia Turner," I sighed, my eyes locked on the ground.

"Emilia Turner, you're under arrest for the kidnapping of Clara Fallon and aggravated assault with a deadly weapon. You have the right to remain silent, anything you say or do will be held against you in the court of law."

I nodded, and was dragged to my feet, unable to miss the horror movie scene before me. Groups of paramedics crouched over Mason and Clara, gurneys, shouts, flashing lights, and blood: everywhere.

I began to cry harder, past and present almost a perfect mirror, mind and body losing the will to function, the dark force wailing alongside the pain pounding throughout the room. Grunts and I was off the ground, the dark-clad arms of police officers blocking my view. *Almost* all of it.

Mason was alone. And yet his face looked tranquil in its isolation. Arms folded across his chest, a crimson halo surrounding his still body, that faint smile still on his face. It was the last thing I saw before being carried into the dead night.

I broke.

22

AFTER

When you're young, you don't think much about death. It's not something that comes up. Death wasn't something I was used to. Something no one should be used to, but that's life. It felt so empty and dark. Without anger to soften the blow or cloud it, it was a special type of painlessness. A numbing sensation far more dangerous than any type of pain.

"Miss Turner?"

Gone. He was really gone.

"Miss?"

And it was my fault.

"Uh... Miss Emily?"

My eyes flashed up, everything snapping back into place as I looked at the speaker. It was clear she was uncomfortable, dark eyes flickering, voice shaking.

"You have a message."

I sighed, trying to push the woman away, but she was persistent. I had already asked about Clara, but no one would tell me anything. I didn't need to ask about Mason. Jonathan had planned for everything. Even trying to stop him had been fruitless.

"It's from the hospital."

We were face to face now, separated only by a row of grimy bars. I could tell she wanted to step back.

"The hospital?"

"Do you want to use your phone call?"

"Was the message from my Mom?"

"Yes."

Seconds later I was searched, then led into a dim room, where a pale landline phone waited for me.

"Hey honey," Mom's recorded voice said, as if everything were fine. **"I'm so proud of you. Remember that, okay? Calling 911, and with the landlord and everything, well... I don't have very long to call. At least that's what the doctors said."** She paused, coughs hacking through the screen, the pain slowly cutting its way back to me.

"**Anyways, they're sending someone to pick you up. Don't worry about me, okay? Stress isn't good for either of us, is it?**" A faint laugh. "**They're saying I have to hang up now, but I'll see you soon. We can get through all this. I have a friend and—okay okay, I know.**" A sigh. **"I love you Emily, no matter what. I—"** Coughs overtook everything, shouts breaking through occasionally, then a crash and silence. A long beep and the message ended.

"Mom?" I gasped, hitting the phone as if it would do any good. I began to scream, at the phone, the officers, the dark-eyed woman, everyone. I was returned to my cell, racked by wails where I collapsed on the ground.

"Miss Turner?"

"What happened to her?! What did you do?"

The dark-eyed woman fidgeted, shuffling the papers in her hands.

"Calling us was the right thing to do—"

"Where is my Mom?"

"Your mother came into the hospital at 4:38, and we... we found something on a scan. She was bleeding badly."

"Was?"

"Your mother passed away, honey. She was suffering from stomach ulcers, which burst and... she didn't make it. I'm so sorry. That message was the last thing she said."

"LEAVE."

More shuffling papers. "I know how tough this must be, but—"

I looked up at the woman, and she stopped. She stepped back and, with a glance behind her shoulder, left.

The world wouldn't stop spinning. I knew my cheeks were wet with tears, snot running down my face, nails cutting into my palms, but even the pain seemed pointless. There was nothing to control the emptiness inside me now. It was so much worse than before.

I can't do this anymore.

I looked around the room, anything sharp would do, something to stop the emptiness, anything to end the pain. But then, it stopped. I was on the ground. I wasn't breathing as the dark fell, that emptiness enveloped everything.

23
DURING

Scratch that. What I did to Peter, so long ago, was… perhaps the beginning of this mess. But in a way it's almost like an ending. Let's go back.

~

"Jonathan," I squeaked. I didn't have the courage to say anything else.

He stared back at me, occasionally looking at Peter. The blankness in his eyes scared me more than what I had just done. That look would haunt me forever.

He tilted his head, eyes never leaving mine as he disappeared back into the alley. Gone again.

When I looked back at Peter, I began to shake. Everything was a blur. Anger, a release, then the crack of a head against asphalt. I hadn't meant to hurt Peter, of course not.

Didn't you? I thought. *You hit him after all.*

"No," I whispered, scrambling to my feet. "Not today."

With a final glance back at Peter, I slipped away, trying to ignore the guilt boiling inside me.

THE EMOTIONS only grew bigger as I ran home, I knew they were dangerously close to overflowing. It was still the middle of the day, and I knew the house would be empty, so I should be safe there.

I snuck inside, checking to make sure no one saw me as I closed the door. I turned, already pulling my shirt over my head when I heard a clatter.

"Emily!" Mom shrieked, rushing past the shattered plate to me. "What happened? Is this your bloo—"

"Don't touch me," I said, ducking past her into my room. "And no, it isn't."

"Emilia," Mom cried. "Did someone do this to you? Talk to me! Oh god I'm calling the cops, I—"

"No no no!" I shouted, flipping around to her shaking face. "Mom, please calm down. Whatever you do, don't call the cops."

"You can't expect me to—"

"Trust me!" I called, looking pointedly at her as I slipped past. "I'm taking a shower. When I'm done, we'll talk."

"Emilia—"

"Please Mom."

She didn't answer, and I prayed to every god I could think of that she'd listened. I was in and out of the shower in minutes, letting the warm water wash away the fear shaking through me. Inhale, exhale. I had to focus. Clean clothes, dry hair, any scarlet gone.

"Mom? Hello?"

No answer.

"I'm out of the shower. Where are you? Mom, I think—"

"Are you Emilia Turner?" a voice barked, hands grabbing mine from behind.

"She is," Mom's voice whispered from behind me. I flipped around, met with a tall man in police attire. Mom hovered behind him, face tear-streaked and puffy. "Is it true?"

"What!?" I shrieked, but I knew it was in vain.

"Peter Lockman?"

"I—"

"There's bloody clothing in the bathroom," another man interrupted from the hall.

I was pushed forward, cold cuffs snapped over my wrists.

"Please, please I didn't do anything, I swear. Mom! Mom, tell them. Stop, STOP!"

As I sobbed, the world spun in and out of focus. Mom's tortured face the last thing I saw before everything went dark.

~

I WAS SENTENCED to one and a half years in Juvenile Detention for what I'd done. Peter lay in a coma for three months as I was on trial, and when he woke up, I guess you could say I was relieved. All I remember from that time was screaming, tears, bright lights, and the haunted faces of other teenagers.

One day stands out to me, though. The day I saw Jonathan again.

~

I DIDN'T RECOGNIZE the boy in front of me. He was familiar, same face, same hair, same voice even, but... changed. He had become cold, angry, violent.

"Hey Em," he whispered, sitting in the chair across from me.

"What are you doing here?"

He laughed, but it was too forced, too fake. "You know what I'm doing here."

I stared. I really didn't. I'd thought I'd seen the last of Jonathan that fateful day. And yet, here he was.

He didn't wait for an answer. "You know what happened that night, right? I called the cops on you, Em. After what happened, I mean, why wouldn't I? I had lost everything..." he trailed off, a darkness falling over his face. He looked up at me again, smiling a too-wide grin. "A week into the investigation, they came to my house. Let's just say they found out what Peter had been doing, and now I'm here, in this hellhole. And it's all because of *you*."

"What you and Peter were doing had nothing to do with me," I whispered.

"No!" Jonathan shouted, jumping to his feet. "No, Em. *You* caused this."

"No, I didn't. You're in here because of what *you* did. I'm sorry Jonathan, but—"

"Fuck you, Emilia," he whispered, a silkiness smoothing his features. "If I ever see you again, it'll be too soon."

The slam of a door, and he was gone, leaving me shocked and strangely empty. I wasn't sure why. Maybe because we ended on bad terms, or maybe because he wasn't the same person I knew before.

When I left Juvie, Mom and I decided we needed a new start. A clean slate, and time to forget. So when we left without a glance back, I knew things would change. For better or worse, I couldn't know.

And yet, I had a feeling this wouldn't be the last time I saw Jonathan Sinclair.

24

AFTER

She was gone.

When I first opened my eyes, I thought I was still unconscious, still trapped in the inevitability of my past.

He had won.

Everything was black. The darkest and deadliest black I had ever felt. It was full, clashing against the emptiness, taunting it.

There was nothing I could've done.

I tasted salt on my lips, something swishing around me, buoying me up. But I didn't care. There was so much I wanted to say, to her, to Mason, to everything and everyone. I could've stopped him, I could've done *something* to prevent what happened, but I didn't. And now it was too late.

Too late, too late, too late.

It echoed inside my head, a pain throbbing and freezing my

body, my mind. I wanted to retreat, to find anything to say to my former self. If I even wanted to, did I?

Did I?

I'm sorry, I would've said, *I love you.* And then... nothing. The words twisted and muddled in my head before disappearing, the emptiness devouring it with an intensity that the dark force couldn't match.

And what did it matter? I was alone and trapped in the darkness and pain and destruction of myself. Although, where was I? The swishing of *some* substance let me know I was awake, alive even?

Was I alive? What did it mean to be alive?

Who was I?

I couldn't remember my name, or my life. Mason, Clara, I knew them. Jonathan.

"Emily," someone said. Was that me?

And then everything burst open, memories flooding from everywhere, how and why Jonathan had done it, although everything felt muddled and dim. It didn't feel *right.* The rest of the memories were sharper, and much more gruesome.

PETER LOCKMAN'S DEATH. He *had* died. That didn't feel right, but it was true. The police storming my house, Mom's face, the pain and betrayal and darkness. Peter had *never* woken up.

I remembered death, blood, triumph, flashing lights, courtrooms, scared faces, and screaming. Dark places, nails bitten to stubs, pain, anger, so *much* anger. How it overflowed. White gowns, needles, electricity, water.

Birthdays passed unceremoniously, pain and emptiness and joy. Twisted joy. Laughing and knives and more blood.

Straps tightened and thrust into a dark box, water exploding over the sides. The feeling of drowning, trapped, nothing to combat the emptiness.

The memories subsided, flickering off like the end of a movie. They were real, that I knew. Crystal clear and highlighted in blinding color. And the rest, Mason, Clara, Jonathan, were grey and dull. They weren't the truth. Lies woven by something, someone, to cope with the horrors she'd been through. The death she faced, the guilt and pain, the dark force inside her. Inside *me*.

How I needed to tell Mom, needed to see her, but was never given the chance.

I gasped, back to the present, the motion pushing me under, water filling my lungs, but being unable to move. Something circling my arms, legs, midsection, head, tightening and restricting me. I couldn't breathe, water feeling like syrup as I struggled against the restraints, confusion, panic, pain, flipping throughout the darkness.

And light.

Splashes and sound, strong arms pulling me out of the water, and sight. Colors at first, dull and cloudy, then shapes and brightening and... people? People clad in white gowns, goggles, gloves, standing before me with confused, angry faces.

I meant to walk, to speak, but couldn't. A newborn introduced to a world she barely remembered.

"Emilia Turner, how do you feel?"

He was the closest, sleeves stained dark with water.

I swallowed, the too-bright lights burning me, the sights, sounds, smells, emotions. Too much.

"Do you remember?"

"Remember?" My voice was brittle and dry, so quiet. I was surprised anyone could hear it.

"How everything—" the man began.

I heard a crash and then a door burst open, a short figure striding into the room. She was clad in dark clothing, unrecognizable. She stopped, throwing the mask off her face.

"Emily."

Impossibly, she stood before me. Frizzy hair, creased forehead, tired voice.

"Mom?" I cried. "Mom, is it really you?"

Her arms were around me, squeezing tight. A warmth curled into being, shining and filling me.

"Mom, I'm so sorry."

"I know," she whispered back, and those words, the feeling—that newness—grew, building and destroying the darkness, the pain, and the emptiness.

Cheeks finally dry, I let myself fall away, a warmth inside me shining faintly for the first time.

A second chance.

I grinned.

THE END

EPILOGUE

March 11 2037
Patient 12HRA7
Dr. Herman Swartz
Subject Report

OBJECTIVE: Patient Emilia Elizabeth Turner was transferred to Emerald Rehabilitation Services in late January, 2036. Our objective was to rehabilitate and reroute Miss Turner's psychopathic tendencies using self-developed, isolation tank hypnotherapy-pharmaceutical methods.

PERSONAL HISTORY: Miss Turner was arrested and convicted for the aggravated assault and manslaughter of Peter Aaron Lockman, at the age of 16, and spent several years in jail, convicted as an adult. Miss Turner was released in 2035, where she began using narcotics and drinking heavily. In 2036, she was found guilty of murdering eight people, as is stated on public record. Miss Turner was assigned to the Placebo Project, her treatment commencing on February 17, 2036.

HYPOTHESIS: We believe we can achieve rehabilitation using hypobenazathenal in conjunction with isolation tank therapy. We expect this therapy will neutralize the archaenil and benazelene in Miss Turner's brain, hiding her unwanted memories, changing her psyche, and enabling her to rejoin society.

RESULTS: Surprisingly, Miss Turner's brain reacted to the hypobenazathenal without external stimuli. Instead of wiping her memories, they were enhanced, creating a fictionalized version of Miss Turner's past, with several significant adjustments. Miss Turner created several characters -- Mason Taylor, Clara Fallon, and Jonathan Sinclair -- in what we believe was a subconscious coping mechanism.

This coping mechanism "re-created" Miss Turner's life, starting with Peter Lockman staying alive, rather than being murdered by Miss Turner. This set many changes in Miss Turner's subconscious life that did not happen in her real life, such as the addition of "villain" Jonathan Sinclair. This person only exists in Miss Turner's subconscious, and alongside Miss Turner's other fictionalized characters (such as Mason Taylor and Clara Fallon) offers essential information on how her brain reacted to the treatment. After studying this new "reality" we've realized each character represents part of Miss Turner's changing psyche.

We believed Jonathan Sinclair represented Miss Turner's darker side and how it came to dominate her for a time, then eventually faded away.

Mason Taylor represented the version of Miss Turner she used to be, one that eventually died, leaving her psychopathic self to gain prominence.

And finally, we believe Clara Fallon represented Miss Turner as she could've been, before all of the trauma. As Clara's fate remained unknown after the simulation, we aren't sure how Miss Turner would've reacted to that.

As Miss Turner continued to spiral out of control, we decided to administer additional hypobenazathenal, which instead of giving us more control, eventually shocked the patient out of the simulation.

CONCLUSION: As we continue to review Miss Turner's fabrications, and how her brain reacted, we realize something has changed. In her final "standoff" against villain Jonathan Sinclair, Miss Turner experienced a loss different than before. Looking over her scans and reactions, before and after the Placebo Project, we believe it was a success. This discovery could eventually improve the lives of hundreds, and hopefully, provide relief to Miss Turner herself.

If you enjoyed *When I Left*, please consider leaving a five-star review on Amazon.

Believe it or not, every review really helps!

https://www.amazon.com/When-Left-Novella-Zoë-Pruden/dp/1956708219/

*(Alternatively, do a search for **Zoe Pruden** in Amazon's **books** subcategory.)*

AFTERWORD

Whoo, we're done! Goodbye countless editing, late night writing, and pondering sentence syntax.

In reality, writing *When I Left* was and is, one of the craziest experiences I've ever took part in. When I first started this daunting project, back in December of 2020 (I know! 2020—two *years* ago), I didn't have any *real* idea what was coming.

I was assigned this venture as a sort of 8th grade senior project, back in Sunfield Waldorf School. I'd been going to Sunfield for the entirety of middle school but until a few years back, I didn't really know what I wanted to do. I'd always loved writing, but to write, finish, and publish an actual book? With a mentor I barely knew helping me along the way? It was a tall order for 13 year old Zoë, someone who clearly underestimated how much work she'd be putting in.

And yet, when I had the idea for *When I Left* (a product of late-night pondering) I absolutely knew I had to do it. The only question, was how.

I met Richard Cox (my wonderful mentor and author himself!) back in November 2020, where we began working on the first draft of *When I Left* in December 2020. It was a rollercoaster of emotions, to say the least. Writing the first draft is like putting your clothes on inside out and living with it. My first draft was riddled with inconsistencies and confusion, and trust me when I say I was a disaster in those several months. But I had to get over this "word vomit" phase and send Richard my chapters. Around 1–3 chapters per week before finally finishing in April 2021.

Then came the intensity of editing, or, I should say, rewriting. Editing is like flipping your clothes right-side up, and realizing you've put your shoes on the wrong feet. After changing this (and your outfits several times as well), it comes together with a sort of patchwork frame.

For me, this came as an entire subplot (flashback storyline), which ended up with me cutting about 8,000 words from the draft. After communicating with Richard, my father, and countless friends, I finally deemed it ready for execution. I smoothed out the cracks to the best of my ability (in reality, I would come back to it in several years later and edit some more) before finishing the night before my deadline. The relief I felt then was cathartic. I turned in my "finished" draft in May 2021, graduating Sunfield with pride.

Two years later, here we are. After really, really, *really* editing this novella, I think I'm finally ready to share it with the world. Two years is a lot for a teenager, especially during Covid, so to say I changed some things would be an understatement. Nevertheless, it's definitely been a rollercoaster immersing myself in this fictional world. Knowing the characters, tweaking the plot, and crafting a story I can be proud of. It's been an incredible experience learning the ins and outs of writing/publishing a novella and I am so excited to see what will come after this. I truly think this experience pushed me harder than anything else, and it's certainly made me the writer I am today.

So. Was writing *When I Left* easy? Not even in one way. But am I proud of myself? Hell yes! It may have taken me a little longer than planned to finish this, but I cannot describe the elation that comes with knowing it's done. This chapter of my life may be over, but I *know* my love of writing is far from its end. This experience has changed my life, and I hope reading *When I Left* may change yours, however small it may be.

Zoë Pruden
Port Townsend, WA
October 6, 2022

Acknowledgements

Many wonderful people not only heavily influenced this novella, but have held me and my story together over the years. I am so incredibly grateful to everyone that's helped with this project, whether editing, reading, or simply giving encouragement!

I'd like to thank my friends and family, who've brought back my ever-waning inspiration and given feedback when I asked for it.

To Richard Cox, my amazing mentor and editor who helped me learn about writing plot, character, and so much more. Without him, I would've burnt out years ago. I couldn't thank you more.

To Sunfield Farm and Waldorf School's Helen Curry, who started me on this path in the first place.

To my proof readers, Ash Madrone, Penny Pruden, Mom, Dad, and more.

Thanks to Tom Jacobs, who has given well-thought advice and last-minute edits, as well as proofreading.

To Dad, who coached me through late night discussions and publishing this book! As my partner in this entire debacle, he's a major part of this process.

And finally, thanks to you, THE READER. Without you, *When I Left* is nothing more than paper and pain.

Finally, one big thank you to everyone that's helped me come this far. I don't even know where I'd be without you. Probably under my covers.

So, thank you.

Zoë P.

About the Author

Zoë Pruden lives in Port Townsend, Washington. An avid bookworm and illustrator, she loves to write, and published her first book—*Alex's Adventure,* a children's book—at age 10. She is a proud 2021 winner of NaNoWriMo (National Novel Writing Month) during which she wrote a science fiction novel centered around the zodiac.

ALSO BY ZOË PRUDEN

ALEX'S ADVENTURE, A CHILDREN'S BOOK

At the age of only 10, Zoë was already writing stories and this clever little children's tale follows the story of an errant cat who finds herself lost, separated from her family and trying to find her way back home.

Filled full of unique lines that only a 10 year old could write, this charming tale is sure to put a smile on your child's face.

LIMITED EDITION COPY

There are only *100 copies* of this limited first edition. Priced at $14.95.

Please contact **ross@rosspruden.art** for sales inquiries.

Made in USA - North Chelmsford, MA
1333627_9781956708219
09.20.2022 1711